The

Diaries

clearwater crossing

The Diaries

laura peyton roberts

BANTAM BOOKS
NEW YORK • TORONTO • LONDON • SYDNEY • AUCKLAND

RL 5.8, age 12 and up
THE DIARIES
A Bantam Book / June 2000

ISBN 0-553-49334-5

Visit us on the Web! www.randomhouse.com/teens
Educators and librarians, for a variety of teaching tools, visit us at
www.randomhouse.com/teachers

Published simultaneously in the United States and Canada

Bantam Books is an imprint of Random House Children's Books, a
division of Random House, Inc. BANTAM BOOKS and the rooster
colophon are registered trademarks of Random House, Inc. Bantam
Books, 1540 Broadway, New York, New York 10036.

PRINTED IN THE UNITED STATES OF AMERICA

OPM   10   9   8   7   6   5   4   3   2   1

This diary belongs to:
Jenna Conrad

If found, do not read!

Dear Diary,

Today has got to be the best first day of school in the history of Clearwater Crossing! I got great classes, and it was fun to see how everyone has changed over the summer. Mostly the changes are about what you'd expect, longer hair and darker skin, a few sun streaks here and there, but Naomi Richards got her nose pierced! I was shocked that her parents would let her, and I'm not even sure why she'd want to, except that she obviously thinks it looks pretty cool. Peter and I had the best time at lunch, talking to friends from last year and finding out what they'd been up to. I just love the whole first day atmosphere—new classes, new clothes, and all the excitement of a brand-new year.

But that's not even the best part. Miguel del Rios is in my homeroom! I can't believe I got so lucky. I <u>have</u> to meet him, and now I'll finally have my chance. He looks just the same as last year, except that right now he's incredibly tan. His eyes are still that same soulful shade of brown, though, and his smile still makes me jelly right down to my toes. Did I say he looks the same as last year?

Scratch that—he looks better! Did I already mention that this was the best day of all time?

Of course, I didn't spend the <u>whole</u> day thinking about Miguel. There's a lot of other stuff going on too. One of the guys on the football team, Kurt Englbehrt, has leukemia and the other Wildcats and the cheerleaders are putting on a carnival this Saturday to help raise money for his medical care. I only know Kurt by sight, but I still felt awful when I found out he had cancer. Everyone says he's getting better, though, and the carnival is a <u>great</u> idea, so Peter and I definitely want to help. I don't know exactly what we'll be doing there, but we'll find out at the volunteers' meeting they're having after school on Wednesday.

I'm so lucky to have a best friend like Peter, who likes to do things like that. He was the one to suggest it, actually, but I'd have volunteered anyway, because it's important to help people out when you can. I realized today that this will be our sixth year as best friends. That's pretty long! You'd think we'd be sick of each other by now, as much as we're together. We see each other at school every day, at church every Sunday, and we almost always get together on Saturdays, too. Ever since Peter and Chris started Junior Explorers on Saturday mornings, we have a little less time together, but I could never complain about such a worthy cause. Those kids need Peter more than I do.

This Saturday, though, since Peter and I are going to be working at the carnival, Chris will have to manage the kids on his own—or, more likely, he'll get Maura to help him. Those two make the cutest (and unlikeliest!) couple. I wonder if they're going to get married soon? Chris is something like twenty now. I would guess they want to finish college first, but you never know! Maybe they'll surprise us.

Well, I should finish writing and hide this before Maggie comes upstairs and finds out I'm keeping a diary. If she knew, she'd only snoop around until she found it and probably read the whole thing. I really wish I didn't have to share my room! Especially with such a messy, noisy, nosy younger sister. She's downstairs watching TV with Allison and Sarah now, but that can't last. If only Caitlin would move out, I could have a room of my own! I still don't understand why she didn't go to college, like Mary Beth, but now that she's graduated from high school, the least she can do is get a job, move out, and give the rest of us some breathing room. I love my sisters, but people grow up—and there are times when a little more privacy would be nice.

Now how did I get off on that tangent? I've wanted my own room forever, so why worry about it right now? It would be a shame to ruin the most otherwise-perfect day of my life! ☺

Oops, I hear Maggie on the stairs, so I just have one more thing to say:

CCHS Juniors <u>Rule</u>!!!

———

Tuesday morning

I only have a second before Peter picks me up, but I'm so excited I can barely wait. Maggie took off ten minutes ago, and how many times can I pace our room without going crazy? I hope Miguel talks to me today. Or maybe I'll find a reason to talk to him. It'll have to be a <u>good</u> reason, though. Chelsea Stephens tried some lame excuse yesterday about not being able to read the board, and it totally backfired on her. Miguel knew exactly what she was up to. He's like that. He's quiet, but you get the feeling he doesn't miss much. I think that's part of what drives the girls so crazy—that and the fact that he's probably the cutest guy at school. Come to think of it, he's probably heard it all in the lame-excuse department, with so many girls chasing after him. It would be fine with me if he was a little <u>less</u> chased after, but that's his only flaw. Besides, so far no one's caught him. ☺

Okay, Peter's going to be here any second, so I'm going to put this away now. I wish I could tell him about Miguel, but I'd be too embarrassed. I've never even told him I have a crush, let alone who it's on. I have to admit there are certain things it might be easier to share with a girl. I really can't imagine Peter sighing over Miguel's swimmer's physique, for example, or that <u>cute</u> little broody face he makes. Peter's my best friend, but he's still a guy. He just wouldn't understand!

———

Wednesday night

Dear Diary,

You will never, <u>ever</u> guess what happened today! Peter and I went to that carnival volunteers' meeting after school and I got the surprise of my life! I want to start from the beginning, though, and write the whole thing down, because I'd hate to forget even a second.

The cafeteria was so packed when we got there that we could barely find places to sit. It made me feel good to see how many people had turned out, because it shows how much our school cares. It probably didn't hurt that Kurt is a popular football player, but I honestly don't believe that was a huge factor—it didn't matter a bit to Peter and me. We finally found a couple of seats near the front just as the meeting was called to order by Hank Lundgreen. (Somehow he ended up this year's football captain instead of Josh Stockton. Oh, well. I don't really keep up with these things.)

Hank yelled for everyone to sit down, then barely paused before he kept right on talking. "Thanks for coming out," he said. "The team's put a lot of planning into this carnival, but we wouldn't be able to pull it off without the help of the cheerleaders, and the support of all of you."

The cheerleaders loved that. They were sitting with the football team off to one side, and all of them cheered like crazy. Not to be cynical, but I had the feeling they were cheering more for themselves than for our great support.

"So, here's the deal," Hank went on. "We've already figured out all the booths and rides and ordered what we need. We're expecting a huge crowd, and we need you people to help us man the booths."

There was already either a Wildcat or a cheerleader in charge of every concession, so Hank started calling them to the podium one by one to say how many helpers they needed. If you wanted to volunteer for that booth, you were supposed to stand up and wait to be picked. Josh Stockton was the first called up. He may not be the football captain, but he's definitely the biggest guy at our school. Josh was in charge of security, but said he only needed a couple more guys, because he was using mostly players.

"Big guys," he had to clarify as people jumped to their feet all over the room. I think all guys secretly believe they're the Terminator. All except Peter, that is.

"I guess that lets me out," he joked, flexing his not-so-big muscles.

He knows he's skinny, but my mom told me that guys who get so tall so fast always thin out from the growth spurt, and Peter must be over six feet now. His older brother,

David, is even taller, but he's not skinny at all. I mean, he's not fat, either. He looks good. Not that I'm <u>looking</u>. You know what I mean.

<u>Anyway,</u> Josh finally choose two guys and took his group out of the cafeteria. Barry Stein was next up. He wanted three volunteers to sell tickets for the rides, and he got at least ten to pick from. Barry and his group left too.

Are you ready? Here's where things start to get good.

The next name Hank called was Jesse Jones, which was a new one on both me and Peter. This tall, brown-haired guy walked up to the podium, along with Melanie Andrews. He said that the two of them had the main food concession, and that they were going to be cooking and serving hamburgers and hot dogs, along with chips and lemonade. He wanted six volunteers. Right away, this one blond girl jumps up like it's a fire drill, practically on her toes to wave her arm in the air. But no one else stood up. Not one other person.

Jesse knew the blonde from somewhere, because he knew her name. "Okay, Nicole," he said. "Anyone else?"

He'd pretty much strutted up to the podium, but you could practically see him shrink as the seconds ticked by and no one else volunteered. He kept looking around the room, at all those people sitting on their hands. Even Melanie looked worried, and she always seems too cool to let anything faze her. I guess if I were that pretty <u>and</u> the only sophomore cheerleader in the history of CCHS nothing much would faze me, either. But you could see her stressing right then.

"No one else wants to volunteer because cooking hamburgers is probably the worst job they've got," I whispered to Peter. "Hot and greasy and plain hard work."

Peter nodded. "I know," he whispered back. "Want to do it?"

It's at times like that I'm so glad he's my friend. I mean, the whole point of the carnival is to help Kurt, so who cares if the job is glamorous? It all has to be done.

Jesse about died with relief when we stood up, and he picked us right away. We were still walking to the front when someone else stood up and Jesse picked her too. I'd seen the new girl before, but I wasn't sure of her name, which turned out to be Leah Rosenthal. She's very pretty too, although in a completely different way than Melanie.

Okay, and here's the best part: <u>The next</u>

person to volunteer was Miguel del Ríos! I was still trying to put a name on Leah, and I couldn't believe my ears when I heard Jesse call Miguel from the podium. I didn't even know he was in the room until that moment, and I was so excited to see him joining us that I actually felt weak. I could tell I had this goofy smile all over my face and my heart was pounding like crazy. If I'd thought about it from now until Christmas, I couldn't have come up with a better way to finally meet Miguel.

That was the highlight of the meeting, of course. No _way_ could anything top that. But our group did end up with one last member. The last guy Jesse picked—the only other person to volunteer—is this nerdy-looking kid with slicked-down hair and horn-rimmed glasses. I thought for sure he was going to land on his face as he stumbled up through the tables, tripping over everything in sight.

"Oh, perfect," Nicole muttered. "It's Screech from _Saved by the Bell_." It wasn't a very nice thing to say, but nobody disagreed. I'm afraid it's pretty true.

"I'm Ben Pipkin," the poor guy said when he finally reached our group. He stuck out his hand to shake, but everyone was so embarrassed that no one wanted to touch him. I wish I could say I'd moved a little faster, but Peter was the first to shake. Jesse never did. And that's when I first started to feel kind of sorry for Ben. It must be awful to have people react to you like that—practically recoiling in horror—but I get the impression he's used to it. That's kind of a sad thing to have to get used to.

On our way out of the cafeteria, Ben tripped over his own sneaker. His arms flew out and all his books went sailing, and he crashed headfirst right into Miguel. Lucky for Ben, Miguel is a lot bigger than he is, and a lot stronger, too. Somehow he managed to grab Ben by one arm in time to keep him from hitting the floor. Everyone in the cafeteria laughed until Miguel finally snagged Ben's other arm and hauled him back onto his feet.

Ben said thanks, but his face was the color of ketchup. Then he dove to retrieve his books right when Leah bent to get them. They smacked skulls so hard that Leah fell over backward, and the whole cafeteria started laughing <u>again</u>. The whole thing was really embarrassing—even <u>I</u> was blushing. And that's when Peter and I decided to be extra nice to Ben. After an introduction like that, the poor kid's going to need all the help he can get.

Outside, Melanie and Jesse filled us in on everything we'd be doing at the carnival, and also where to show up, and when. All I can say is, I hope Peter was paying more attention than I was, because I was staring at Miguel the entire time. I still can't believe I'm going to spend <u>all</u> <u>day</u> with him this Saturday! Even though there are going to be six other people there, if I can't find a way to talk to him <u>sometime</u>, I might as well give up now.

Ha! Not likely. I've been waiting for a chance like this ever since I was a freshman!

Wouldn't it be great if we finally got together?

———

Thursday

Dear Diary,

~~Someone famous ought to write a book about how to survive in a house with five sisters. It would be really inspiring to know that a star grew up under these conditions and everyone turned out normal. If I find one more piece of Maggie's dirty laundry on my side of the room~~

I'm really going to try harder not to say (or write) negative things. Starting from this page forward, I'm going to focus on the good—and if I accidentally forget and write something negative, I'll just have to scratch it out. It kills me to mess up such a nice book, but you know what they say: Thoughts turn into words and words turn into actions and actions turn into character (or something like that). In any event, negative thinkers become negative people. Besides, I love my family—more than anything. Only a baby would expect things to be perfect all the time.

Instead of complaining, I ought to concentrate on how <u>lucky</u> I am to have five sisters. What if I'd had five brothers instead? I wouldn't like being the only girl. Besides, when we were all younger, before Mary Beth left for college in Nashville, we used to have some terrific times. Once Dad got us a cabin and we all went fishing up at Clearwater Creek. Mary Beth convinced us girls to wade out to the big rock in the middle one morning before Mom and Dad were even awake. We were going to catch enough trout for our breakfast—or at least that was the plan. Mary Beth was forever cooking up schemes like that. She's always been the most adventurous, but then again she's the oldest, so it kind of makes sense (Maggie would give her a run for her money now!). Anyway, Mary Beth went first, and Caitlin followed, holding Sarah's hand so tight she probably squeezed all the blood right out of it. Sarah was really little then, and scaredy-cat was terrified she might slip and drown or something. Looking back, I don't even know how Mary Beth talked Cat into coming, but they were really tight then, and Mary Beth always could make her do anything. Anyway, I followed Caitlin, then came Maggie, then Allison. We would have all been in order of age if Sarah hadn't taken cuts. We had barely put worms on our hooks, though, when Mom crashed onto the bank, panicked out of her mind because she'd woken up and found us missing. She wasn't too happy about everyone being out in the middle of the creek, either, but Dad calmed her down. The funny thing was that after all that fuss, we only caught one little fish. Mom cooked it up anyway, and everyone got about one bite each on a plate full of warm buttered corn bread with honey, with huge mugs of steaming hot chocolate. That must have been the best breakfast ever.

The next time Maggie leaves dirty laundry on my side of the room, I'm going to think about that. ☺

———

Dear Diary,

I am <u>so</u> excited! Tomorrow is the carnival. At lunchtime Peter and I were at our favorite table in the quad when Melanie and Jesse walked up and said they wanted to have one more meeting of our carnival group after school. I thought we had settled everything on Wednesday, but of course I didn't argue about another chance to see Miguel! ☺

We all gathered behind the cafeteria, and that was when I realized that meeting again had been Jesse's idea. Melanie didn't seem too happy about it at all. In fact, when he told us that he wanted us to dress up Hawaiian-style at the carnival, she came pretty close to losing her temper.

"You called a meeting for that?" she said. "I'm going to miss my bus for <u>that</u>?"

"No problem," Jesse said. "I'll give you a ride home."

Maybe I read too much into it, but I thought

she gave him a pretty dirty look. "I don't mind dressing up if everyone else wants to," I said quickly, just to smooth things over.

"I could go either way," said Leah, and Peter didn't care either.

"Well, I think it's a <u>great</u> idea," Nicole said. "It will make our booth stand out from everyone else's. What do you think we should wear, Jesse?"

He still seemed kind of flustered by Melanie's reaction. "I don't know," he said. "Maybe the guys could wear Hawaiian shirts, and you girls could get hold of some grass skirts or something."

"Oh, there it is!" Melanie snapped. "With coconut halves on top, I suppose. You'd like that, wouldn't you, Jesse?"

The rest of us just stared at her. I mean, her tone was really harsh. I guess that's when I first realized that she and Jesse aren't really friends. They're only working on this carnival thing together, like all the rest of us.

Jesse swore that he didn't have any ulterior motives. He said he'd only hoped that having a theme might attract more customers, so that our booth could make the most money for Kurt, and I guess she finally believed him. I know <u>I</u> believed him.

"All the money's going to the same place," she said. "It doesn't matter who makes the most."

"You're right," Jesse admitted. "I'm just competitive, I guess. But after all, if a thing's worth doing, it's worth kicking butt at. Right?"

"I don't think it matters what we wear," Miguel said, obviously as eager to end the argument as I was. "Let's just agree to the Hawaiian idea, and everyone can do it however they want."

"I can borrow my dad's Hawaiian shirt," Ben said. "He and my mom went to Oahu for their anniversary, and he got this really cool one with pineapples and—"

"That's good, Ben," Jesse interrupted. He makes it really clear how little he thinks of Ben. It's all in the way he rolls his eyes. "Now, who wants to meet me here early to set up the tarps and grills?"

Ben and Peter signed up for that, and then Nicole offered to bring some tropical decorations to spruce up the booth with. I suggested we could give ourselves a funny name and put it on a sign.

"Oh! Oh! I know!" said Ben. "What about Team Take-out?"

Everyone laughed, so that's our name now.
We may be eight near-total strangers, but
together we're the mighty Team Take-out.
Or does mighty sound too silly? No, Team
Take-out's the part that sounds silly.

Anyway, after the meeting broke up,
I almost had a chance to talk to Miguel.
Melanie took off in a big hurry, and Jesse
followed, still saying he'd drive her. On second
thought, maybe Jesse likes Melanie all right,
but she definitely doesn't like him. I wonder
why not? <u>Anyway</u>, there was this moment
when Miguel was standing by himself at
the edge of the lawn. He could have just gone,
but it almost seemed like he was hesitating
on purpose, maybe hoping to strike up a
conversation. I was just about to walk over
there when all of a sudden he turned around
and walked off. He didn't even say good-bye.
I could have caught him, but Peter was there
and before I could move he said we should get
going because he had a lot of homework to
finish, since we're spending all day tomorrow
at the carnival.

Oh, well. I don't know what I would have
said to Miguel anyway. But I do know this—
I can't <u>wait</u> till tomorrow!

Dear Diary,

What a lot I have to tell you! First off, the carnival was a huge success. At our booth alone we made a thousand dollars. Then this morning, at church, our congregation took up a special collection for Kurt, which can only help even more. I'm getting ahead of myself, though, because I want to write about the carnival first.

Me, Leah, Melanie, and Nicole were all supposed to get to the school gym early to make the lemonade from scratch. Leah, Melanie, and I had been squeezing lemons quite a while, though, before Nicole finally showed up. Because of Jesse's Hawaiian idea, I was wearing a Hawaiian shirt with my chinos, Leah had on a flowered halter top and shorts, and Melanie was wearing a Hawaiian-print dress. Even so, none of us could believe it when Nicole ran into the gym wearing a skimpy bikini and a plastic grass skirt that didn't cover anything. I know I'm more modest than most people, but I could tell Melanie and Leah were pretty shocked too.

Come to think of it, there's probably even a law about serving food with that much skin exposed.

Poor Nicole. I felt really sorry for her. I mean, Jesse _did_ say grass skirts, so she was just trying to do what he wanted. When she saw the rest of us, though, and realized she was going to be the only one, she got totally red in the face. Nicole's eyes are the brightest blue I've ever seen—that turquoise kind of blue they still can't fake with contacts. They're the first thing you notice about her anyway, but with her cheeks all pink like that her eyes stand out even more—and right then they looked completely panicked. I was so glad I had an extra Hawaiian shirt in my backpack. I brought it because I thought someone might need it if they got spilled on (probably me), but Nicole needed it right then. She said she had some shorts in her car, so she ran off to put that stuff on while the rest of us finished the lemonade.

When we got out to the football field, the guys had already set up most of our booth, and did it ever look good! We helped by hanging up the signs Leah had made, and then everyone went wild taping on streamers and puffed-paper pineapples. By the time we had finished, there was barely a minute before we were supposed to open, but Peter and I couldn't resist running around for a quick peek at the rest of the carnival. They had booths on both sides of the football stadium, and with all the different-colored tarps, tablecloths, and items for sale, the whole thing looked like a patchwork quilt on a grass-green background. Our booth was near the entrance, but there was tons of other food: candy apples, peanuts, popcorn, caramel corn, cotton candy (my favorite!), and warm, gooey cinnamon rolls from that place called Hot Buns downtown. The rides were in a fun zone in the gym parking lot, and they even had a Ferris wheel. Peter and I made plans to ride that later, but we never found the time. Not that I'm complaining! I was having so much fun that by the end of the night I'd forgotten all about it. ☺

Which is _not_ to say that working the booth was easy. We had to hustle like crazy, and at times we got so busy we could barely keep up. Probably the worst thing that happened was when Ben spilled a big vat of lemonade on everyone. Later he squirted ketchup all over himself, and he kept dropping people's change in the grass all day long. He's the biggest klutz I've ever seen, but he seemed truly sorry every time he messed up. The <u>best</u> thing that happened was when Kurt stopped by our booth with his girlfriend, Dana. We were all excited to see him—especially Jesse, since they're on the football team together. I was working the counter then, so I could hear every word when Jesse and Melanie called Kurt and Dana over. At first Dana stayed outside the booth, smiling but looking stressed, even though Kurt's supposed to be getting better. I really felt for her. She looked pretty scared to me.

"Hey, Jesse! Thanks for coming out," Kurt said.

"It's good to see you here," said Jesse. "I didn't know if you'd be coming or not."

Kurt seemed surprised. "Are you kidding? I wouldn't have missed this for anything! It's incredible what you're all doing for me."

That's when Jesse seemed to remember that he wasn't doing everything all by himself, and he pushed Melanie forward. "You remember Melanie, right?" he said.

"Who doesn't?" Kurt said. He had a point—the whole school knows Melanie Andrews. "Hey, Dana!" he called. "Come say hello."

She didn't want to, but she finally came around the tables and said hello to Jesse and Melanie. Then she turned back to Kurt. "It's getting dark and you need to rest. Let's go find your parents, okay?"

"Since I've been sick, Dana acts more like my mom every day," Kurt teased.

"I'm sorry," Dana said, explaining to Melanie. "I try not to worry, but he's my best friend and . . ." She got so choked up she could barely finish. "Well, you know how it is."

Then I got choked up at the mere thought of losing my best friend. I can't even imagine what I'd do if it were Peter who had leukemia. But Melanie stayed as calm as if the two of them were discussing a TV rerun. ~~That girl must have lemonade running in her veins.~~

"Sure. I understand," she said coolly. "He's lucky to have you."

"I sure am," Kurt agreed, putting his arm around Dana's shoulders. "I couldn't have gotten through this without her."

"You're not through it, Kurt," Dana said shakily.

"Ah, come on, Dana. You know I'm going to beat this thing."

But Dana kept insisting he ought to go home and rest, so we all dropped what we were doing to run over and meet him before he left. That's when I got a huge surprise.

"Miguel!" Kurt said, catching sight of him for the first time. "I didn't see you back there at the barbecues! How's it going?"

They shook hands, and then they hugged! Judging by everyone's faces, the rest of the group was as surprised as I was to realize that those two knew each other. Since Miguel had never said anything, we were all under the assumption that _Jesse_ knew Kurt best. Nicole said Jesse just moved here from California last spring, though, so aside from the fact that they're both on the football team he can't know Kurt that well.

When Miguel stepped back, Peter and I had a chance to say hello. Peter told Kurt he was sorry about his leukemia, but glad to hear he was getting better, and then he introduced me. From a distance, Kurt doesn't look _too_ sick, but up close you can see how bad off he is. His skin is pale and yellowish, and all his veins show through it. My heart kind of skipped a beat—until I noticed his eyes. Kurt looks sick, and he looks weak, but he definitely doesn't look beaten.

"I want you all to know how much I

appreciate your support," he said. "It's been overwhelming."

"Our pastor is going to take up a special collection at church tomorrow," I told him, excited. "I know our congregation would help in other ways too, if there was something we could do."

Kurt seemed truly touched. He reached for Dana's hand and pulled her closer, then stood blinking back tears. "You could pray for me," he said at last.

That really humbled me, to see faith like that after all he's been through. Maybe I shouldn't say this, but I really hope I'm never tested the way Kurt has been. If that's what God has in store for me, though, I'll be glad if I show even half as much courage. And you bet Peter and I are going to pray for him—we'll pray like crazy!

Today we took the special collection at church, and I really liked the verses Reverend Thompson read (Matthew 25: 34–40):

> Then the King will say to those on his right, "Come, you who are blessed by my Father; take your inheritance, the kingdom prepared for you since the

creation of the world. For I was hungry and you gave me something to eat, I was thirsty and you gave me something to drink, I was a stranger and you invited me in, I needed clothes and you clothed me, I was sick and you looked after me, I was in prison and you came to visit me."

Then the righteous will answer him, "Lord, when did we see you hungry and feed you, or thirsty and give you something to drink? When did we see you a stranger and invite you in, or needing clothes and clothe you? When did we see you sick or in prison and go to visit you?"

The King will reply, "I tell you the truth, whatever you did for one of the least of these brothers of mine, you did for me."

I've heard those verses before, but today they hit me in a special way. And I still feel on top of the world every time I think about the difference we made for Kurt. I'm actually sorry the carnival's over. It would have been fun to keep going, to keep helping somehow. We had a pretty good group, really. And now that

I've had a chance to spend some time with them all, here's what I think about the members of Team Take-out.

1. <u>Miguel</u>: I like him more than ever! You could tell he was genuinely glad to be able to help Kurt, and he worked really, really hard. I wonder how they know each other?

2. <u>Jesse</u>: He's pretty nice. A little bossy, maybe, and awfully sure of himself, but I know he was just worried about our group doing well. By the end of the night he'd relaxed a lot.

3. <u>Ben</u>: What can I say? He tries.

4. <u>Leah</u>: I think I like her best of all (except for Miguel, of course ☺). She's so nice and really easy to talk to.

5. <u>Melanie</u>: She's nice too, but a little bit standoffish. She doesn't act snobby or anything, but there was a part of me that felt like I needed a <u>reason</u> every time I talked to her. Maybe I was just being insecure because she's so popular. Not that popularity is important, or that I'm in awe of it or anything. I don't know. I spent a whole day with

her and I still don't feel like I know her at all.

6. <u>Nicole</u>: She's nice. Although I couldn't help noticing that she was a lot nicer to me than to Ben. Of the guys, she clearly prefers Jesse.

That's only six people, but Peter and I make up the other two, and obviously my opinion of us hasn't changed!

My only little regret is that I never got to spend any real time with Miguel. I was working at the front counter almost all day, and he was cooking back at the barbecues. It doesn't matter, though, because what we were doing was way more important. Besides, now I'll have all kinds of conversation starters when I see him in homeroom tomorrow! ☺

———

Monday night

Dear Diary,

I talked to Miguel today! Not that we had a real big conversation. We were both in homeroom a few minutes before Mrs. Wilson, and I asked if he'd done the geometry problems she'd assigned on Friday. He had, so we compared answers. That wasn't cheating, because we both did our own work. And even though I changed one of my answers to match his, and he changed one to match mine, that <u>still</u> wasn't cheating, because we found our own mistakes and fixed our own papers. Mrs. Wilson never said we couldn't help each other.

After that, we started to talk about the money we'd raised for Kurt, but by then the room was filling up and everyone was making so much noise it was hard to carry on a conversation, our chairs being in different rows and all. Still, it was a start. My heart was racing the whole time, and Miguel smiled at me before he turned around in his seat. I could barely think about anything else the rest of the day!

Well, I'd better wrap up for now. Peter's coming over and we're riding our bikes down to the park. He's still trying to figure out something to do with the Junior Explorers this weekend and I think he's hoping that cruising the activities center will inspire him. He's been there nearly every Saturday for the last two years, so I don't know what he thinks he'll see that he hasn't seen a hundred times before. If he wants to ride down there, though, I don't mind. The weather outside is <u>gorgeous</u>. I think fall must be my favorite time of year.

Oops, there he is. Got to go.

———

Tuesday

Dear Diary,

Kurt Englbehrt is in remission! I'm so happy! Between the chemotherapy and the radiation he's been getting, all the cancer is gone from his body. Now he just has to get his strength back up. Pretty soon his hair will grow in again, and before long he'll be as good as new. It's like a miracle. Everyone's calling it an answered prayer, and that's what I believe too. No one at school was talking about anything else today, and even having Ben spill orange juice all over me at lunchtime couldn't dampen my good mood. (Get it? Dampen? ☺)

It's just such unbelievably good news! I feel so thankful about it that I'm not even going to mention what a pigsty Maggie's side of the room is. I mean, I'm not going to mention it to <u>her</u>. Not that it would help if I did. Lately it seems like the more I complain, the messier she gets.

But I refuse to think negatively! Seeing Kurt, and realizing that even people my age can get sick, has made me really grateful that no one in my family has ever had anything too awfully wrong with them. We're really lucky, and I'm going to concentrate on that. ☺

———

Wednesday

We made banana bread in home ec today. It was so good that I'm pasting the recipe in here, to make sure I don't lose it.

Banana Nut Bread

Ingredients
¾ cup shortening
1½ cups sugar
3 eggs
3 cups all-purpose flour
¾ tsp. baking soda
¾ tsp. baking powder
¾ tsp. salt
3 very ripe bananas
¼ cup sour milk
½ cup chopped walnuts

Instructions

Preheat oven to 350 degrees. With an electric mixer, mix together shortening and sugar. Add eggs and beat well. Add dry ingredients (the next four) and mix just until stirred in (don't put all the flour in at once or it will fly out everywhere). Add bananas and sour milk and mix until the bananas are thoroughly mashed up and incorporated. (If you don't have sour milk, make it by putting a tablespoon of lemon juice in a measuring cup and then adding milk to the 1/4 cup line.) Put the nuts in last and mix just until distributed. Scrape batter into a 9 1/4 x 5 1/4 x 2³/₄-inch ungreased loaf pan and bake approximately 90 to 105 minutes, until the whole top of the bread rises up and turns a very deep golden brown (usually with a crack across it). Fully cooked bread won't jiggle when the pan is shaken slightly.

So good!

Dear Diary,

Maggie is over at a friend's house, so I have our room all to myself for a while. I don't have anything very important to write, but I feel like I ought to take advantage of such a golden opportunity. Well, on second thought, I could be writing an English paper for Mr. Smythe, but ~~he gives me the biggest pain in the~~ there's plenty of time to get to that later.

Actually, I did like a poem he brought to class the other day. The class is supposed to be creative writing, but he's forever wanting us to read things written by famous writers, things we students could never hope to measure up to. ~~I really think he likes to torture~~ He sets the bar a little high. Anyway, this one was by William Wordsworth and it's called <u>Intimations of Immortality</u>. It's really long, so I'm just going to copy out my favorite part:

Our birth is but a sleep and a forgetting:
The Soul that rises with us, our life's Star,
Hath had elsewhere its setting,
And cometh from afar:
Not in entire forgetfulness,
And not in utter nakedness,

But trailing clouds of glory do we come
From God, who is our home.

Isn't that beautiful? It gives me chills
every time I read it. And I really like it when
teachers aren't afraid to discuss something
like that, that deals with the subject of God.
I mean, everyone believes <u>something</u>, even if
they believe God doesn't exist. But a lot of
teachers are so reluctant to talk about God that
if you went by what you learn in high school
it wouldn't be hard to conclude that nobody
believes anything. Most of my teachers would
rather talk about sex than religion, and you'd
think sex would be twice as touchy.

Hey, so there's something <u>positive</u> I can say
about Mr. Smythe! He loves the old religious
poems, and he's not afraid to talk about them.
~~Then again, he's not afraid to talk in general.~~
Man! I was so close.

———

Saturday

The CCHS football season is off to a great
start. The Wildcats won their first game
last night, and Jesse was practically the star
player. Peter and I always go to the games, but

we've never really been friends with a player before. It definitely makes things more exciting! We murdered the Muskrats, and when Jesse caught that final, leaping pass, I nearly screamed myself hoarse. Melanie was there too, cheering with the squad. She's the smallest of the eight cheerleaders, so when they do the pyramid she's on top. Kurt E. came out on the field and waved to a standing ovation. We even saw Nicole, sitting down the stands from us with a girl named Courtney Bell. Peter and I had Courtney in English last year, but I didn't know Nicole knew her. Courtney's kind of loud—the type of person who's always rolling her eyes if you say something she doesn't agree with. She doesn't agree with much. I don't really ~~like~~ understand her. Anyway, she and Nicole seem pretty close, so I guess I ought to keep an open mind.

This morning I was going to help Peter with the Junior Explorers, but he said he didn't need me because all the kids were going to do was paint. My mom was practicing piano, so I went downstairs and sang with her awhile instead. It's twice as fun being in choir now that she's the choir director, and tomorrow we're going to sing at least two of my favorite hymns. I still can't wait for Christmas, though. The Christmas songs are my favorite. Besides, it just _feels_ different somehow, being in church at Christmastime.

After practice, I helped my mom bake a pie for tonight's dinner. Apple—yum! I wish we could eat it now, but dinner's still hours away. I guess I'll log on to the school Web page and see what's new in the guest book. Ta ta!

———

Sunday night

Dear Diary,

I am _so mad!_ The City Council is backing out of its promise to buy a new bus for the Junior Explorers. Peter told me about it during our picnic today after church. He didn't spring it on me right away, though, so at first I was having fun. The weather still feels more like summer than fall, and since it was Peter's turn to bring our lunch, I was really hoping he brought cookies. His mother is a cookie-baking genius.

"I brought grapes, too," he said, pulling this squishy, steamy plastic bag out of his backpack. I know fruit's supposed to be good for a person, but ick.

"What kind of cookies did you bring?" I

asked (which maybe wasn't too tactful). They turned out to be Oreos. I definitely prefer his mother's, but of the store brands Oreo cookies are best.

We were eating our sandwiches when he told me about the bus problem. The Junior Explorers used to have this decrepit old school bus that someone donated when the program first started. But it barely limped through last summer and died at the end of August. Without the bus, Peter and Chris can't afford to take the kids on field trips or, worst of all, to the two-week summer camp they've held upstate the last two years.

"Chris found out last night that the funding for the replacement bus fell through," Peter told me.

"You're kidding!" I cried. "How could it?"

"Budget problems," he said. "I don't know."

"But they can't do that!" I insisted. "Don't they know the kids are counting on that bus?"

Peter laughed to see me getting so fired up. "Maybe we should send you to the next council meeting to explain it to them."

"Oh, I'll explain it all right!" I said, really mad by then. "We ought to all go down there and explain it."

"I don't think it would do any good," Peter

said. "Chris told me the money's just not there."

"But they <u>promised</u>!" I insisted. I just couldn't let it go. "And the old bus was already junked."

Peter sighed. "I know," he said. "The kids are going to be so bummed."

"You aren't going to tell them!" I said. "It'll break their hearts if they don't get to go to camp this summer."

"What else am I going to do?" he asked. "I can't exactly buy them a new bus out of my allowance. I wish I could."

"Just don't tell them yet, okay?" I said. I admit I don't know how, but I have to believe that the money will be found somehow. It will just be too awful if it isn't. I was still trying to figure out another source of funding when Peter changed the subject.

"You know who stopped by the park and helped us paint yesterday?" he asked. "Melanie Andrews."

Somehow I couldn't quite imagine sophisticated Melanie Andrews making dripping tempera paintings with a bunch of little kids. "What was she doing there?" I asked.

"Just riding her bike through the park when she saw me making a mess of things. She's a really good painter. She and Amy painted this whole ocean scene with palm trees and waves and little sand castles."

I know it's stupid, and immature, but I don't much like the idea of Melanie helping out with the Junior Explorers. I mean, if Peter needed help, why didn't he call me? For that matter, I _offered_ to help and he said he didn't need any. But what he said next bothered me more.

"You know, Melanie is an interesting girl," he sighed, all moony, with this faraway look in his eyes.

"Oh, please! Not you too!" I begged.

That snapped him out of his little dream. "What's the matter with you?" he asked. "I thought you liked Melanie."

"I do. It was just nice to know one last member of the male species who didn't live and breathe for Melanie Andrews, that's all."

"You can't be serious!" he said. "Me and Melanie Andrews? Yeah, that'll happen." The mere idea seemed to crack him up. He laughed and laughed until I felt kind of stupid—but kind of better, too. "That wasn't what I meant," he finally got out.

"Then what _did_ you mean?" I asked.

His eyes got distant again. "I mean, she's different," he said. "You should have seen her with the kids. I think she's lonely."

"_Lonely!_" Now it was my turn to laugh. "Melanie Andrews! You're nuts." She's the most popular girl in school! Guys follow her around everywhere.

"Maybe," he said. "But I don't think so. There's just something about her."

"Well, I never noticed it," I said. "And the next time you need help with the Junior Explorers, I wish you'd call me instead. Melanie has all the friends she needs without taking one of mine."

Peter made a goofy face. "That's really going to happen. You know you're my best friend, Jenna."

That was all I wanted to hear. As far as I'm concerned, she can show up at his house every morning and help him tie his shoes now.

I just hope he really _doesn't_ have a crush on her. Peter's a great guy—she'd be lucky to get him. But girls like Melanie don't generally date guys like Peter.

I just don't want to see him get hurt.

———

Dear Diary,

I had a fight with Maggie today, and I am really upset with myself—especially since the more I look back on it, the more opportunities I see to have just walked away. At the time, though, I was really furious, and all my good intentions went right out the window.

I was trying to do my geometry homework, and I wanted to get it done early so I could watch <u>Angels Among Us</u> after dinner. All of a sudden, Maggie waltzes in and starts bothering me for no reason. She didn't have any homework, and apparently she didn't have anything else to do, either. She put on that stupid CD by that stupid band Clue (and I'm <u>not</u> going to cross out "stupid" because that's not negative—it's just a fact). Then she plopped down on her bed and started singing at the top of her lungs. She can sing without breaking glass if she wants to, but today it was like she was howling off-key on purpose, just to get my goat.

"Maggie, I'm trying to work," I said, pretty calmly under the circumstances.

She just gave me this big, fake grin. "Who's stopping you?" she asked.

"You are," I said. "Why don't you go do something useful, like help Mom with dinner?"

"I already did all of <u>my</u> chores, Jenna," she said, all snidely, "which is more than you can say. It's your turn to clean our bathroom."

That only irritated me more, because she was right and I'd forgotten all about the ~~stupid~~ bathroom. Since Caitlin, Maggie, and I share one, I only have to clean it every third week, but we're supposed to do it on the weekend. There was no way Mom was going to let me watch TV with that chore still not done—which only meant that the homework time Maggie was wasting had just become even more precious.

"I'll tell you what," I said. "Leave now and I won't smash your CD player."

I would never actually do that—I was only trying to make a point. It was the wrong thing to say, though, because it made things worse.

"I'd like to see you try!" Maggie said, jumping up with her hands on her hips. She's starting to look just like Mary Beth when she does that (M.B. when she was younger, I mean). They both have those same too-tight auburn curls and masses of freckles. More importantly, they have the same stubborn streak.

"Just get _out_ of here, Maggie," I said, losing what little patience I had left.

"It's my room too. I'll stay if I want," she shouted.

"I have to have quiet!" I shouted back.

"Then go downstairs," she said. "There's no one in the living room."

I'll tell you what—I really wish I had. Instead I yelled some more, and she yelled back. Then I made fun of her lifelong crush on Scott Jenner, and finally she stormed out. I really thought I'd won until Mom came into our room.

"Jenna Elise Conrad!" she said. She could have quit right there. You know you're in trouble around here when Mom uses your middle name. "You still haven't cleaned that bathroom?"

"I'm going to, Mom. I'm just finishing my geometry homework first." I meant to sound calm and reasonable, but instead my voice came out all whiny. Why does that always happen at the worst possible times?

"Don't worry about geometry," she said.

"You'll have plenty of time to finish it tonight, when you're _not_ watching TV."

So now everyone else is downstairs watching <u>Angels Among Us</u> and Mom was right—I've got plenty of time. Maggie won after all.

The weird thing is, I don't even feel like watching anymore. That's my favorite show and I don't even care about missing it. I just wish now that when Maggie decided to annoy me I hadn't made things so easy for her. Who knows? Maybe she wasn't even <u>trying</u> to annoy me. I could have been nicer. I could have been more mature. I <u>could</u> have gone to the living room. I really do want to be a good person. I try my hardest. But things happen, and sometimes I mess up. <u>You</u> try living with five sisters.

———

Tuesday night

Dear Diary,

Kurt Englbehrt is dead. It's the most horrible thing. I still can't believe it. When we got to school today, all the homeroom teachers had to read a memo from Principal Kelly saying that Kurt was killed in a car crash last night. He was driving alone. He died alone. I've been crying all day.

Nobody understands why it happened. I mean, if he'd died of leukemia, everyone would have been really sad, but to have him get well and then die in such a senseless accident is somehow much harder to take. My entire homeroom was crying—guys too. Even Mrs. Wilson. Miguel buried his face on his desk and wouldn't even look at me. It's the most awful thing that's ever happened at our school. By far.

Everyone was so shocked and upset that I honestly think they should have closed the school after homeroom. Because the more people talked about Kurt, the more upset they got. And no one was talking about anything else. When lunchtime finally came it was a relief to be with Peter. He didn't understand why it had happened either, but he was absolutely positive God hadn't abandoned Kurt. Peter's faith is really deep. Sometimes I feel embarrassed, like mine ought to be as strong, but mostly I just appreciate the way he props me up when I need a little help. Seeing him today felt like latching on to a rock in a storm—and I wasn't the only one who thought so.

We were still in the cafeteria, talking over by the door, when a totally amazing thing happened. Melanie left her table with the cheerleaders and started walking over to us. Peter turned around, their eyes kind of met, and then she started running. The whole place went silent, watching. I really had no idea what was going to happen, and I have to admit I was pretty surprised when she threw herself into his arms, sobbing like her heart would break. I mean, why did she choose Peter over all her other friends? And why then? Why there, in front of everyone? I guess Peter was right about Melanie after all. Even with all those people around her, she's lonely. It's like there's something missing in her life.

We took her outside as soon we could because everyone was staring. I mean, Melanie is usually so cool and today she was a total mess. I have to admit, I liked her for it, though. It's good to know that inside that perfect shell she's as human as everyone else. Once she pulled herself together, I think she was embarrassed. She said she didn't know what had come over her, but that her mother had died in a car accident too. Kurt's death must have brought back that pain again. I felt so sorry for her, and now I'm really glad that I got the chance to meet her. It just goes to show that you never <u>really</u> know a person until she cries on your shoulder.

CCHS is having a memorial service for Kurt after school tomorrow. It seems awfully sudden, but I guess they think it will help us deal with what's happened. Peter and I will definitely go, but right now I'm going downstairs to be with my parents. We're all going to pray for Kurt.

———

Wednesday

Dear Diary,

Kurt's memorial service was really sad, but I feel like something good came out of it too. At least I feel better than I did yesterday, and I don't think I'm alone.

They held the ceremony out on the football field. In a way that seemed like a weird choice, since Kurt's carnival was on the same grass not even two weeks ago. But he was a football player, so I guess he would have approved. The school built a big platform with white bunting directly beneath one goal post. Peter and I were standing in the crowd out in front of it, waiting for things to get started, when Ben wandered over and joined us.

"This whole thing is so depressing," he said. "I can't believe Kurt's gone."

"It was a horrible accident," Peter agreed. He didn't add the obvious, which is that <u>nobody</u> can believe it.

"Yeah," Ben said. "But it's not just that. I mean, even when he was sick, I don't think anyone ever believed that Kurt would die. How could he? He was just a teenager! And then the way he finally went . . . just driving like that . . . completely sober . . . It could have happened to any of us." We were all still thinking about that when Leah came over.

"I'm glad someone I know showed up for this thing," she said. "I wanted to come, but it's hard to listen to something so sad by yourself."

Peter nodded and checked his watch. "Have you seen Melanie today?" he asked.

"No, but there's Nicole," Leah said, waving her over.

If Leah hadn't pointed her out, I'm not sure I would have recognized her. She looked <u>terrible</u>. Nicole usually likes very trendy styles, but today she was wearing faded jeans, a baggy T-shirt, and sunglasses so big they covered half of her face. Her hair was greasy and limp, and her face looked totally washed out. It took me a couple of minutes to realize that I'd never seen her without makeup on before. We called her again and she finally came over, moving in slow motion.

"Are you okay?" Leah asked her.

"This hasn't exactly been the best week of my life," Nicole said with a shrug. I shouldn't have been surprised, because we were all hurting, but I still wouldn't have expected Nicole to take Kurt's death the hardest. I don't want to sound harsh, but up until today she's always seemed a little, well, self-involved. I felt bad to see her so low, but at the same time I was really glad to find out I'd misjudged her.

Then Melanie showed up. She was wearing sunglasses too, but aside from that she looked as cool as ever, as if that scene in the cafeteria yesterday never happened. It was almost weird, because we'd never planned to all meet up that way. In fact, I don't think any of us had ever expected to hang out together again. But there we all were.

"Aren't you supposed to stay with the football team?" Peter asked her.

"I don't feel like it. Besides, what are they going to do to me?" she said.

"No, stay with us," I broke in. "It seems right for us all to be together. After all, it was Kurt who brought us together the first time."

"Only we're not all together. We're still missing Jesse and Miguel," said Peter.

"I doubt Jesse will disappoint you," Melanie said, kind of sarcastically. No sooner had she spoken than Jesse burst out of the crowd and hurried over.

"What are you doing here?" he asked her. "The team is all supposed to stand together."

Melanie shrugged. "So sue me. I'm not in the mood for fistfights today."

I don't know what she was talking about, but Jesse looked pretty embarrassed. "I <u>knew</u> you were mad about that," he said. "Listen, Melanie, I wasn't going to fight with Nate, but the guy was being a total jerk."

"You, on the other hand, behaved like a prince," she said, even more sarcastically.

And then Nicole started crying.

"Could we please not argue?" Leah told them. "Nicole is upset, and you two aren't helping."

"Sorry," Melanie murmured. "Sorry, Nicole."

Jesse acted as if he'd just that second seen the rest of us. "Oh, hi, everyone," he said nervously. "I didn't realize we were all back together."

"Except for Miguel," Ben said. If he hadn't said it, I would have. I mean, that's a pretty big omission.

"I wouldn't hold my breath," Leah said. Before I could ask why not, the Englbehrt family came out on the dais with Hank Lundgreen, Coach Davis, and Principal Kelly. Then Dana Fraser walked up to the podium, looking shaken and frail in a plain black dress. I felt sick just watching her, especially since every time she opened her mouth to speak, she got choked up and had to stop. I can't even imagine what it would feel like to have my boyfriend die. Miguel's still barely a friend to me, and the thought of him being in Kurt's shoes makes me want to pass out.

"This isn't how it was supposed to happen," Dana managed at last. "I figured if I ever stood up to make a speech to y'all about Kurt, it would be because he'd been elected Homecoming king, or won a football scholarship, or at least kicked all your butts on the SATs."

People laughed, but only to help her along. I can assure you that nobody felt very cheerful.

"I can't say I know why Kurt died. And it's doubly hard when we were all so excited about the future," Dana got out, right on the verge of tears. "But what I really want to say is that I loved him—_really_ loved him. And I know a lot of you did too. I have to believe that counts for something. I think it's true what they say, that love never dies."

Then she started crying for real, and Hank had to help her to a seat beside Kurt's family. I was crying too, and if Peter hadn't been there to hold my hand, I probably would have started bawling. After Dana, Coach Davis took the podium, and that was when I noticed that Miguel had slipped into our group. Normally I get this jolt anytime I see him, but I was just too sad today. Besides, the more I stood there thinking about it, the less sense it all made. I mean, of all the people at school, why did _Kurt_ have to die? He probably had more people praying for him than any one of us.

I think we were all relieved when the service was finally over. Everyone was crying and trying to act like they weren't. The crowd started breaking up and leaving, but all of us from Team Take-out just stood there like we were frozen in position.

"I feel awful," Nicole said at last. So did I. On top of saying good-bye to Kurt, I think we had all just realized that was probably the last time we'd ever be together as a group, so now we had to say good-bye to each other, too. It was funny how no one was in a hurry to do that, because we don't have a lot in common, but we did make a really good team.

"You know what the worst thing is?" Ben asked. "The worst thing is that it's over."

Nicole shook her head. "I don't think I could have stood it if those speeches had been any longer."

"Not the memorial," Ben said. "The hope. Two weeks ago we didn't even know each other, but we came together to try to help Kurt, and for a while there it felt like we'd really accomplished something. Now we know we didn't. That's the worst thing. Knowing that it's over and we didn't make a difference."

"Yeah. I know what you mean," Jesse said.

"Sorry, but I don't," Peter said. "I think we _did_ make a difference. Not the difference we wanted to make, I'll grant you. But aren't you glad now that we had the chance to do one last thing for Kurt? I've got to believe he's going to heaven with a big smile on his face, just thinking about all the people who loved him. Kurt had faith, and so should we."

I wanted to applaud. I thought he'd said it just right, but some of the others seemed pretty skeptical.

"Still," Leah said. "We all know what Ben means."

"Maybe," Peter said. "But maybe it _isn't_ over."

"What do you mean?" Nicole asked. "Of course it is."

"Not if we don't want it to be," Peter told her. "Ben said he wanted to make a difference for Kurt, and I think I know a way we can do that."

"How?" Ben asked.

"Let's do something to honor Kurt's memory. Let's not _let_ it be over."

"What could _we_ do?" Melanie asked. From the blank stares Peter was getting, that seemed to be the question on everyone's mind.

"I don't have anything particular—" he started, and then I got this _brilliant_ idea.

"What about the bus for the Junior

Explorers?" I said, jumping in. "We could do fund-raisers to earn a new bus for the kids, and then donate it in Kurt's memory!"

"What kids?" Leah asked me.

"What bus?" Melanie asked Peter. "I didn't see a bus."

"That's because the old one died," I explained. "The city was supposed to pay for a new one, but they went back on their promise and now the kids won't be able to go on trips or to camp or anywhere."

"That's horrible!" Melanie said. "They can't do that."

"I'm afraid they already did," Peter said. "But a bus costs a lot of money. I was thinking a little smaller, like maybe a scholarship prize."

"Oh," I said, pretty disappointed.

Then all of a sudden, Melanie spoke up. "I'll do it," she said. "I don't care how long it takes." I could have kissed her!

"Me too," Ben said with a grin. "I can probably wedge it into my busy social schedule somehow."

Jesse dragged his feet a bit, but eventually he spoke up: "If everyone else is going to do it, I might as well do it too."

"Not to be difficult," Leah said, "but what exactly are Junior Explorers?"

"The Junior Explorers are kids I work with from disadvantaged families," Peter told her. "A few are foster kids, some have only one parent, and none of them have much money. Me and my partner, Chris Hobart, teach them games and crafts and have a good time with them. In the summer we run a free camp. If it weren't for the Explorers, most of these kids wouldn't be able to afford any of the things we do. I hate to sound like I'm pushing my own program, but it really is a worthy cause."

Leah thought another few seconds. "Okay. Count me in," she said.

"That's so great!" I exclaimed. "Everyone's going to do it!" Except I'm not dense. Of course I realized that the single most important person still hadn't said anything. "Oh, wait," I said, trying to be all casual. "What about you, Miguel?"

"Why not?" he said with a shrug.

"That's everyone!" I shouted. But I was wrong.

"Excuse me," said Nicole. "I didn't say I'd do it."

I was pretty stunned. I guess I'd just

<u>assumed</u> Nicole would help, as upset as she was about Kurt.

"Oh, come on, Nicole," said Leah. "Don't break up the group."

"Please, Nicole?" said Peter. "It won't be the same without you."

With everyone ganging up on her, she didn't have much choice. So now we're all going to meet at Peter's house tomorrow night to figure out how to do this thing. I mean, buying a bus is a pretty big deal—I'm not even sure <u>how</u> big, quite honestly. But I know we can do it if we just keep the goal in mind. After all, there must be some reason God brought the eight of us together. ☺

———

Thursday night
Dear Diary,

I can't sleep. As excited as I was about our carnival group staying together yesterday, I'm twice that depressed tonight. You'll never believe what happened. I still can barely believe it myself.

We had that meeting at Peter's house tonight, in the Altmanns' living room, and everyone showed up. Peter and I had the love seat, and Miguel sat <u>right</u> across from me, on the sofa with Leah and Ben. I smiled at him and he smiled back. I actually thought it meant something. Then Peter started the meeting.

"Okay. Here we are," he said, looking really nervous. "I guess we all know what the goal is, right? We want to buy that bus for the Junior Explorers." Everyone nodded, and Peter relaxed a little.

"We'll need to start looking around for a good used bus we can buy," he went on, "but we already know it's going to cost a lot of money. In the meantime, I think we ought to start some fund-raisers to get the cash coming in."

"It seems to me like the first thing we ought to do is figure out where we're going to put the money," Leah said. "I vote that we kick in ten dollars each and open a savings account."

"Good idea," said Melanie. "We ought to have a treasurer, too, to be in charge of deposits. I nominate Peter."

I seconded that right away, and Peter was voted in.

"What about a president?" Jesse asked. "And a vice president? And a secretary?"

"There are only eight of us," said Nicole. "You make it sound like we're starting a club."

I didn't really understand what she was getting at, except that maybe she didn't want things to be so formal. "I don't mind taking notes if you all want me to," I said. "I was going to anyway."

Miguel smiled at me again, and I was so completely, _stupidly_ thrilled. I could tell right then that something big was going to happen. If only I'd known what!

"You ought to write down that the group is opening a bank account," Ben told me, leaning over to point to my steno pad. I started a brand-new one tonight, and I'll keep it for all of our meetings. I made that note, but something about the way Ben said "the group" gave me a new idea.

"We ought to have a name," I said. "We can't go around calling ourselves 'the group' all the time."

"What kind of name?" Melanie asked.

"I don't know," I admitted. "I just this minute thought of it. How about New Beginnings?"

Melanie made a face and asked what that meant. I did my best to explain.

"It's just that something ended when Kurt died," I said. "But in a way, now we're starting over again in his memory. Kurt's life ended, but our coming together to form this group is sort of a new beginning."

"More like a beginning and an ending," Nicole corrected. "I only signed up for this until we earn that bus for the kids. That's what you all said, remember?"

"Maybe we should pick something a little more temporary-sounding," said Leah. "I think Nicole is saying we have more of a pact than a club."

"Exactly!" Nicole exclaimed, obviously relieved.

Personally, I'm not sure what the difference is, or why it even matters. But I wanted everyone to be happy, so I tried again.

"Okay," I said. "Then how about CYA, for Christian Youth Association?"

Jesse snorted. "I always thought CYA stood for Cover Your—"

"Never mind!" I interrupted. I could tell just by the look on his face what he was about to say. "Bad idea."

"And anyway," Miguel said, sounding a little annoyed, "who said anything about this being a Christian group? Leah isn't Christian."

"Neither am I," Melanie said quickly. "I mean, don't get me wrong, I don't have anything against it. But I didn't realize you all wanted this to be a church group. I guess I don't belong here."

She actually got off the sofa arm to leave, and Jesse stood up to go with her. I felt <u>terrible</u>. I mean, I know the whole world isn't Christian. I don't know what I was thinking.

"Wait! That wasn't what I meant at all," I said. "Melanie, please stay."

Lucky for me, Peter rushed to my defense. "I think it was just the type of project that made Jenna come up with that name," he said. "Christians are supposed to help people, so it seems like a Christian project to us. We didn't mean to imply that everyone else has to believe what we do."

See how he said "we"? At least I can still count on Peter.

"It doesn't bother me," Ben piped up from the couch. "I'm a Christian."

Jesse shot him a withering look. "So am I, Ben. That's not the point."

Melanie stared at Jesse as if she were utterly shocked.

"I don't go to church very often," he muttered. "Anyway, you don't have to be a Christian to do a good deed," Miguel grumbled from the couch. "That's ridiculous."

"Of course not," I agreed.

"It doesn't bother me," Leah said. "I don't have a problem with religion." For some reason, she looked at Miguel when she said it. But he never said that _he_ wasn't Christian. I honestly don't know what was going on. It was like I popped open a soda and it turned out to be Pandora's Can.

"I don't have a problem with it either," Melanie said. "I just don't believe it." She finally did sit down, though, so Jesse sat down too.

Then, surprisingly, Melanie grinned. "When you think about it," she said, "it's actually kind of weird that we met each other at all. I mean, we don't have much in common."

"It was Kurt who did it," Nicole said. "None of us would be here right now if it weren't for him."

"I would. I live here," Peter joked.

"No, Nicole's right," Leah said. "This group feels more like something we were chosen for than something the eight of us chose. I guess you could call us Fate's Eight."

"Or how about Eight Mates?" said Miguel.

Leah raised her eyebrows at him. "I meant mates like in Australia. You know—buddies. It's not . . . oh, forget it."

"I think we should call ourselves The <u>Great</u> Eight," Jesse said. I don't want to write anything that I'm going to have to cross out, but that type of remark is pretty typical for him.

"Eight Friends," I suggested, trying to write down everyone else's ideas too.

"If all of our meetings take this long, we'll be calling ourselves the No-Dates Eight," Nicole grumbled. She seemed surprised when we all laughed, but I don't know why. It <u>was</u> a joke. Wasn't it?

"Why don't we just settle on The Eight?" Melanie said. "That's the part everyone seems to agree on."

For a moment it looked like that would be our name, but then Ben burst out with a new idea. "I've got it! Eight Prime!"

None of us had a clue how he came up with that.

"A prime number is a number that can't be divided," he explained. "It can only be divided by itself. Well, by itself or by one—but when you divide eight by one, you still have eight."

"Eight isn't a prime number," Leah pointed out. "It divides evenly by two, or by four—"

"But that's why we'll be Eight _Prime_," Ben insisted. "We'll _make_ it a prime number. We'll be the eight who can't be divided. You know . . ." He leapt to his feet, put his hand over his heart, and made a goofy face. "One number, indivisible, with liberty and justice for all."

I liked it a lot, and so did everyone else.

"I think it's the perfect name," Leah said. "It shows that we're committed. No one can divide us but us."

"It's fine with me," said Jesse, leaning back in his chair. "I always knew I was prime."

You see what I mean about Jesse? Melanie rolled her eyes, so I have a feeling she's noticed the same tendency.

We had barely agreed to the name when Ben announced he had an idea for the first fund-raiser, too: a car wash this Saturday morning. I thought that would be a problem, since Peter meets with the Junior Explorers then, but he wanted to go ahead and do it.

"I think it would be great if the kids help us," he said. "I know they'll probably be more trouble than help, but I want you all to meet them. Besides, it will be good for them to do something to help earn this bus—they'll appreciate it more that way."

"Having all those cute little kids with us won't hurt when we're trying to get people to stop, either," Melanie said.

"Yeah, and that way we'll get Chris to help too," Peter said. "And probably Maura, if we ask her."

A moment later everyone was shouting out things we'd need, like soap, and buckets, and towels. Nicole offered to bring an old cash box and some starter change. We decided to hold the event at the park, since it's a good location for flagging down traffic. Besides, the kids are already there.

That pretty much ended the meeting. Most people grabbed a couple more of Mrs. Altmann's cookies, and then they started to leave. From Peter's living room window, I watched as Melanie and Jesse drove off, Jesse at the wheel of his red BMW. Nicole left right behind them, peeling out in the opposite direction. Leah, Ben, and Miguel lingered, talking on the sidewalk, until a car pulled up and Ben climbed in. I saw him go, but my eyes were glued to Miguel. I still thought it was so amazing that he and I were going to be in this group together. I was even foolish enough to believe that now I'd have all the time in the world to get to know him and, hopefully someday, go out with him.

That's when Miguel opened the passenger door of his car, and I suddenly realized he must have driven Leah to the meeting. She moved to get in, then stopped, still talking.

"What's so fascinating out there?" Peter asked behind me, stopping in the middle of cleaning up the living room. I was so intent on Miguel and Leah, he almost gave me a heart attack.

"Nothing," I said quickly, turning my back on the window.

"I'm going to take these plates into the kitchen," he said. "Back in a minute."

I waited until Peter was out of the room, then turned to the window again. Leah was standing behind the open passenger door, her back to the car. Miguel leaned forward from the curb, a hand on the roof on either side of her. Their bodies were almost touching. Their faces were _so_ close. And that's when I finally got it. The horrible realization of what was about to happen was still just breaking over me when he lowered his face to hers and _kissed_ her.

It felt like one of those try-to-scream-and-find-out-you're-completely-paralyzed nightmares. Especially since that kiss obviously wasn't their first. I spun away from the window already starting to cry. I just couldn't believe it. I didn't _want_ to believe it. Of all the people in the world, why did he have to pick Leah? It's not like she betrayed me, but with as much as I was starting to like her it still felt like a double slap in the face.

Peter came back into the room and noticed I was upset, but I denied it. I was still trying to figure out how I was ever going to face Leah and Miguel again, let alone be in this long-term bus commitment with them. The last thing I want is for anyone else to find out I had such a stupid, futile crush.

No one will _ever_ know how I feel about Miguel. I'll never tell anyone. Not even Peter.

This Diary is the
Private Property of:

<u>Nicole Christine Brewster</u>

(Heather, if you touch this, you're <u>dead</u>!)

Friday

This has got to go down in history as the worst week of my life. For that matter, this whole school year has been awful. After all the weight I lost over the summer, I really thought junior year would be different. But obviously I didn't lose <u>enough</u> weight. The only girl Jesse sees is stupid Melanie Andrews. Not that I can even look at him now, after the way he treated me Monday, like <u>I</u> ought to apologize to <u>him</u> because he got drunk and made out with me at Hank Lundgreen's party last weekend.

I was completely humiliated. First he told me he doesn't like me, then he said it was nothing personal. Nothing personal? It felt personal to me! I must have gone through a roll of TP crying about it in the girls' bathroom. I mean, I've had a crush on him for so long and he just <u>used</u> me. Not only that, but everyone at the party saw us kissing, and that kind of gossip travels fast. I'm such an idiot—I can't believe that I was actually looking <u>forward</u> to having the whole school know what happened. I really thought it was a sealed deal, that Jesse and I were a couple now. Maybe the fact that he was barfing by the end of the night should have tipped me off. I mean, I did realize he was extremely drunk. But I didn't know everything was going to change the minute he sobered up. I <u>definitely</u> didn't know he was going to blow me off in front of half the football team.

I guess I got what I deserved for being dumb enough to believe that someone as great as Jesse could actually like me. I wish that made it hurt less. And that was just the tip of this lousy week's iceberg. The whole school is still reeling from Kurt E.'s death. It just happened so fast, and even though we held the memorial service I don't think people have absorbed it yet. I am so glad it's Friday so I can get away from everything for a couple of days. I mean, I still feel really bad about Kurt, but I just can't talk about it anymore.

If only I didn't have to help out with that stupid car wash tomorrow! As soon as I put this diary away, I'm going to call Courtney and ask her to go with me. She won't want to, but maybe I can talk her into it anyway. She ought to know I wouldn't ask if I wasn't desperate. I don't want to face Melanie and Jesse on my own. I already look like enough of a loser without being stuck there with no one to talk to. The way Jesse follows Melanie around like a lovesick puppy I won't be talking to him. I <u>sure</u> won't be talking to her. Jenna and Peter are so tight they'll probably be together all day, and <u>no way</u> am I hanging with

Ben. Miguel barely ever says two words, so maybe Leah and I could be a team, but I don't want to take any chances. I'll be happier if Courtney's there.

Happy. That's a good one. I was <u>happy</u> when Jesse kissed me. I'd be <u>happy</u> if that situation had turned out the way I thought it was going to. All I really want is a boyfriend, like any normal girl. But sometimes I think no guy is ever going to like me. It doesn't matter how much weight I lose, or how I wear my makeup, or even how I dress. Because <u>I'm</u> not good enough, inside, and I think somehow they sense it.

Wow, that's an encouraging thought. Way to pump yourself up, Nicole.

❀ ❀ ❀

Saturday

Well, here it is, Saturday night, and I don't have anything better to do than sit home and write in my diary. How pathetic is that?

We held that car wash today, and I did get Courtney to go with me—but not without a lot of complaining. "Look at all those little kids!" she groaned the second I pulled Dad's car into the lot at Clearwater Crossing Park. "We're going to end up baby-sitting!"

"I told you the Junior Explorers were going to help too," I reminded her. But I have to admit I hadn't realized there would be so <u>many</u> of them—or that they'd be so out of control. Still, what can you expect from a bunch of first- and second-graders?

"Whoa! Who's <u>that</u>?" Court asked suddenly, sitting straight up.

She was gawking at this completely cute brown-haired guy, who was clearly too old to be in high school. I guessed he must be Chris Hobart—Peter's partner in the Junior Explorers—and I turned out to be right. But Court just rolled her eyes at the sound of Peter's name.

"I suppose it's too much to hope that the God Squad didn't come today," she said sarcastically, checking her hair in the rearview mirror. Peter and Jenna were in English with her last year, and Courtney really dislikes them now because she said they were constantly bringing up Christianity (which means they probably mentioned it once). As far as Court's concerned, having a religion is stupid, but discussing it in public is unforgivable. The fact that <u>my</u> family goes to church every Sunday has never shut her up in the slightest.

"Courtney . . . ," I warned. She was supposed to

be there to <u>spare</u> me embarrassment, not cause me more. And I really don't want Peter and Jenna to find out what she calls them.

"Oh, all right," she relented. "I said I'd be nice to them, didn't I?"

We climbed out of the car and walked toward the entrance to the parking lot, where everyone was gathering. I was carrying a folding card table and the cash box I'd promised to bring, and with the sun beating down on my head it didn't take me long to wish I'd worn shorts instead of jeans. Everything the other members of Eight Prime had volunteered to bring was already laid out on the grass—hoses, buckets, towels, sponges. I headed toward all the junk and Courtney followed behind me, carrying nothing, of course.

Jenna spotted us and came running over. "Nicole! Hi! Let me give you a hand with that," she said. Her long hair was pulled into a high ponytail, but at least she was wearing jeans too. Between us we set up the card table under a big oak tree, with that rusty old cash box Dad gave us on top.

"Great! You got the box," Jenna said, opening the lid to look inside. "And starter change! We should count how much money is in here so we can pay you back afterward."

"Actually, that's my parents' donation to the

cause," I told her. "They said we should keep it, along with the box."

Then Courtney cleared her throat like she had a porcupine in there or something. That was her subtle way of reminding me that I hadn't introduced her.

"Jenna, do you remember Courtney?" I asked. "I think you two had a class together last year."

Jenna smiled. "English, right?"

"Yeah," Courtney said. "You and your friend Peter always sat in the front row."

"That's right," Jenna said, apparently flattered that Courtney had remembered. Of course she couldn't realize that in Courtney's scheme of reality only dweebs sit in the front. Then Jenna's sister Maggie ran over and told us the car wash was about to start. A minute later, Peter whistled everyone over.

"I guess we're starting now," I said.

"Yippee," Courtney replied—like she was the <u>only</u> one who wasn't thrilled to be there. We'd barely walked halfway to the group, though, when she completely changed her tune. "You didn't tell me Miguel del Rios was part of this bus thing!" she whispered, all excited.

"I didn't know you knew Miguel," I said, but my eyes were glued to Jesse and Melanie. They hung back on the fringes while everyone else pressed closer to Peter. Melanie always looks perfect, and I have to admit that Jesse looked good too, even in grungy old cutoffs.

"Please!" Court said. "<u>Everybody</u> knows him. The guy's a total babe!"

"Look, do me a favor and don't hit on Miguel," I begged as we slipped into the group. "I've got to be able to face these people again next week."

Courtney smiled and said, "I'll grant your wish, but only because I'm already busy with Jeff tonight. Otherwise, there's no way I'd promise you something so selfish."

I have to admit it hurt hearing her say the word "selfish." She was only kidding, but the truth is I <u>have</u> been a little too self-involved lately, getting all stressed about guys, and diets, and parties when I ought to be thinking about bigger things. That's the main reason I joined Eight Prime in the first place—that and the fact that everyone totally begged me.

"Anyway, I'm glad to know there are some normal people here too," Courtney said. "At least not <u>everyone</u> in the group is a dork."

She was looking right at Melanie and Jesse when she said it, which I have to admit irritated me. It didn't seem very nice of her to say those two aren't dorks when she knows how mad at them I am. Courtney still refuses to believe that Melanie's responsible for the way Jesse dumped me. But I believe it. And Court's my best friend—she ought to support me!

Then Peter called for attention. "Okay! Chris and the Junior Explorers are going to walk up and down the grass at the edge of Clearwater Boulevard and wave cars into the parking lot. When they come in, try to make them line up where we can reach them with the hoses."

"Are we going to work in teams?" Ben Pipkin asked.

That was the first time I'd noticed him since we'd arrived, and I could have died on the spot. He was wearing the same heinous Hawaiian shirt he subjected us to at Kurt's carnival, but with these baggy, <u>plaid</u> Bermuda shorts. The guy's legs are like sticks, too. Pale, hairy sticks. I couldn't even look at Courtney—I know what she had to be thinking. I just can't <u>stand</u> hanging out with people who don't know how to dress! I mean, Court and I spend a lot of time reading magazines to keep up with the latest trends, but some people don't put any thought into their outfits at all. Not to brag, but I know I have a pretty good sense of style. I don't expect everyone to be as on top of things as I am. But still, a little basic color coordination goes a long way. If you don't know what you're doing, stick to jeans and T-shirts. You may not look exciting, but at least you won't embarrass yourself—or any of the people who have to stand around you.

Anyway, Peter said we didn't need to assign teams, and that everyone should just pitch in wherever. We were supposed to charge five dollars per car and put the money in the cash box. He asked if everyone was ready, and all the kids started cheering.

"I can barely wait," Courtney muttered.

At first things went pretty well. Courtney and I worked as a team, and even though I got stuck with most of the dirty parts while she checked out Chris and Miguel, I didn't complain. I mean, it was worth it just to show certain perfect-looking people that I have friends of my own— I don't live and die by what they think of me. We worked with one of Jenna's sisters for a while— Caitlin, I think her name was—but she was so quiet it was like working with a mute. Then she left and Peter and Ben came over. We washed a couple of cars together and having four people on a team was a definite improvement, but my teeth were on edge the whole time, waiting for

Courtney to make some sort of crack to Peter. If she ever calls him or Jenna the God Squad to their faces I'll die. Luckily, she was too distracted by Ben's outfit to think about anything else.

"You could stand him up in the hardware store and use him as a human paint chip," she whispered as he hosed off the other end of a car. "He must be wearing every color there is."

"And yet, I <u>still</u> don't see one I'd want to paint my walls," I whispered back.

If Ben knew we were laughing at him, though, he never let on. He's actually not a bad person—he's just such a <u>geek</u>!

I was tired by the time Peter and Ben rotated off to work with Jenna. My arms were already aching, and then Courtney and I got stuck with this huge, filthy van. We really needed some help, but we did <u>not</u> need help from Melanie Andrews, who was the one who came sauntering over.

"Do you need some help? Amy and I are between jobs at the moment," she said, smiling down at her Junior Explorers buddy instead of us.

"Yeah. Grab a sponge," Courtney said, without even <u>asking</u> me! I couldn't believe my ears. She <u>knew</u> I didn't want anything to do with Melanie Andrews.

"No, that's okay," I said. "We've got it under control."

"You do? Wouldn't it be easier with more people?" Melanie asked, like I'm an idiot, or I don't know what I'm talking about or something.

"No," I said.

"Yes!" said Court. "Don't be ridiculous, Nicole."

I couldn't believe she'd embarrass me that way. "Courtney!" I said.

"What?" she said, all innocence. But she <u>knew</u> what.

"Never mind!" I said. I threw my sponge down into the bucket and stalked off across the parking lot hoping I'd splashed them both. I didn't even know where I was going. I ended up walking all the way across the lot and then I didn't know what to do, so I kind of stood behind a tree and watched them. They kept right on working together, jawing like old friends, which only made me madder. I mean, I know Court just wants to get in good with her because Melanie's practically the most popular girl in school. It could only help us out to be able to say we're her friends. But I'm <u>not</u> friends with her, so Courtney shouldn't be either.

I was getting ready to march back over and break things up when Jesse and Ben started working on the van too. Of course I couldn't go then, with Jesse right there. As soon as the van was done, though, Courtney wandered off and I snagged her. "Some friend you are," I said. "You better not have told her anything about me."

Courtney swore they were mostly just washing the van. But then she said that Melanie doesn't even like Jesse. I don't know how she found that out washing the van. Besides, I don't believe it for a second.

Everyone was wet, dirty, and tired by the time the car wash was finally over. I got to count the money, and we made $315. The kids had gone home by then, but everyone in Eight Prime was still there to hear our profit.

"That's not very good!" Jenna said, clearly disappointed.

"It's sixty-three cars," Leah said. "I think that's pretty good."

"It felt more like a <u>hundred</u> and sixty-three," Jenna grumbled. "I'm exhausted." A few people snickered, but I agree with Jenna. Washing cars is way too much work for too little money.

"We knew this wasn't going to happen over-night," Ben said. I have a feeling he'd love it if it took the rest of our lives. What else does he have to do?

"We just have to have a little faith," Peter said. "Pass the cash box, Nicole!"

We did that at the carnival, passing it around the circle after we counted the money we'd made for Kurt. It was kind of a spontaneous thing then, and afterward I think we all felt like more of a group. I don't know if it worked this time or not. It didn't work for <u>me</u>. It was getting late, and Melanie and Jesse were standing right across from me, and all I could think about was that in a few minutes they'd be driving off and doing who knows what together.

"Well, I guess that's all for tonight," Peter said. "I'll put this into our bank account."

"When are we meeting again?" Melanie asked, like she's in charge of scheduling.

"Thursday night? My house?" he answered.

Everyone agreed before we broke up, and Courtney and I left first, so I didn't see, but I'll bet you Jesse and Melanie left together. Courtney said if they did it would only be because Melanie's fifteen and doesn't have a driver's license yet, but what kind of lame excuse is that? Ben's fifteen too, and I don't see <u>him</u> catching rides with Jesse.

Oh well. At least I don't have to see any of them tomorrow.

❀ ❀ ❀

Sunday

Well, I only have a couple of minutes because we're leaving for church as soon as my mom finishes getting dressed, but my little creep of a sister is driving me crazy. She wants to go to Sunday school early again, so she can flirt with her teacher. I swear she's in <u>love</u> with the guy, and she's only thirteen! Instead of humoring her, Mom ought to take her to a shrink. ~~If she~~

I forgot what I was going to say up there because Heather just barged into my room and I had to get rid of her. I <u>hate</u> the way she's always doing that! She's in here so much you'd think she didn't have a room of her own. And she comes in for the lamest reasons! Just now, for instance, she said she wanted to make sure I was ready to go. She <u>knows</u> I'm ready—she just saw me when we were all downstairs eating breakfast. When everyone else was eating breakfast, that is. I mostly pushed a slice of cantaloupe around my plate and tried to look like I wasn't hungry. Heather was too busy stuffing her face to comment, for once, and Mom and Dad didn't notice. Sometimes it's really hard to stay on my diet. On days like this, when I'm starving, I dread sitting at the table and watching people eat.

The only thing that would be worse would be if Mom caught on and starting making me eat real meals. Then I'd gain back all the weight I've lost, and

I can't <u>believe</u> it! The little monster was in here <u>again</u>! I swear one day I'm going to have to kill her. Maybe I should start planning now.

<u>Four Completely Silent Ways to Kill Heather</u>
1. I could sneak in at night and hook a pillow over her retainer.
2. I could slip cyanide into that stash of cookies she thinks no one knows about.
3. I could hold her underwater in the bathtub (with the added bonus that maybe her hair would finally get clean).
4. I could seal up her doors and windows and let her suffocate in her own gases!

Sunday afternoon

Well, maybe it's because I went to church today, but suddenly that list I wrote before doesn't seem as funny (except for the part about Heather's gases). I mean, I said I was going to try to be a better person, and I have a feeling God wouldn't think too much of a list like that, even if I <u>was</u> mostly kidding. So, in the spirit of self-improvement, I not only take it back, but I'm going to make a new list.

<u>Five Good Reasons Not to Kill Heather</u>
1. Because "Thou Shalt Not Kill" is one of the commandments.
2. Because it's against the law.
3. Because Mom and Dad might get mad.
4.
5.

All right. I'm sure there <u>must</u> be five reasons, but that's all I can think of right now. I'll have to get back to this later.

❊ ❊ ❊

Monday
I lost another pound! I think it's my new diet. If it keeps on working this well, maybe I'll sell it to <u>Modern Girl</u> for their magazine. The whole thing works by cutting out foods that start with CH. It's almost like someone planned it, how many bad foods start with those letters. CHeese, CHips, and CHocolate, for starters. Those are my big three no matter what diet I'm on. Of course, when you eliminate the CH foods you end up losing chicken, but I can live with that. I mean, who really <u>craves</u> chicken?

On the other hand, if I changed it to just plain C foods, I could pick up Cake and Candy. Or maybe it should be CH and CA foods: CHeese, CAke, and CAndy. I think I may really be on to something.

I didn't see Jesse today, except for a glimpse in the quad during lunch. I hate it the way my heart still races every time I lay eyes on him. I hate it that I still want him, even after the way he acted! Don't I have any self-respect? I ought to walk away and never look back. But if he's really _not_ with Melanie . . . I don't know. I'm pretty confused.

I think Court and I are going to the mall after school tomorrow, so hopefully I'll find something cool to wear on Wednesday. A new outfit always cheers me up.

Oh, great. Now I'm looking back at what I just wrote and wondering if that means I _am_ really shallow. I don't want to be shallow, but honestly my head is starting to hurt just from thinking about it so much. Is this really how someone like Jenna lives, dissecting every little thing she does? I mean, life's short. I can't believe we're supposed to be miserable the entire time.

Tuesday night

Well, you are never going to believe what happened at the mall today! I actually have some good news. Courtney and I went shopping, like we'd planned, and we'd barely even gotten there before Court said she wanted to go into U.S. Girls. The first thing I saw, hanging right inside their door, was this big red, white, and blue poster. Here's what it said:

<u>Are You a U.S. Girl? We Want You!</u>

It turns out their clothing chain is having a modeling contest—and anyone can enter!

"Courtney, look!" I said, my eyes still glued to the poster.

" 'Are you a U.S. Girl?' " Courtney read sarcastically. " 'Help us launch our new line of U.S. Girls jeans by participating in our nationwide model search. Missouri hopefuls compete in St. Louis. Details inside.' So?" she said. "What about it?"

"Wouldn't it be fun to enter?" I asked. I was so excited about it that my mind was running wild. I could practically see myself walking a runway in U.S. Girls jeans, maybe with a rolled red bandanna in my hair. And what if I <u>won</u>? My entire life would change for the better. So of course Courtney had to pop my bubble.

"You're not serious!" she scoffed. "No offense, Nicole, but that's a <u>national</u> contest. Besides, I've got a big picture of your parents letting you drive all the way to St. Louis to compete. Do yourself a favor and forget it."

I think I said I would, but that was just to get her off my case. No <u>way</u> am I going to forget it! The minute Court wandered off to look at clothes, I got an entry blank off the counter and stuffed it into my back pocket before she could catch me. I didn't need to worry, though. Court was so engrossed with the sweaters that she wasn't even watching.

"What do you think of this one?" she asked me, holding up an apple-green angora and smoothing it over her chest. Court always likes to make sure people can see her chest—she's pretty proud of the way things turned out up there.

"Is that your color?" I asked uncertainly.

Courtney smiled and that's when I noticed the sweater was the same shade as her eyes. "If a redhead can't wear it, who can? I'm going to try it on," she said.

She went into a dressing room, and of course I seized the opportunity to check out the new U.S. Girls jeans. They only have three styles, and it's obvious which ones would be best for the contest—the seventies retro pair with the buttons up the fly and the little buckle in back. I grabbed a couple of sizes off the rack and went into the dressing room next to Courtney.

"How's the sweater?" I asked through the partition.

"Jeff's going to like it," she answered, with obvious satisfaction. "It's right up his alley."

"I didn't think you'd been dating the guy long enough to know what was up his alley," I said, trying not to sound as bitter as I felt. I want to be happy for her, but it's hard not to be jealous. Especially since she met Jeff Nguyen at the same party where Jesse kissed me—and things turned out so much better for her. Why couldn't <u>Jeff</u> have turned out to be the jerk? It's not like she's been obsessing over him since last spring, the way I have about Jesse. She'd have gotten over it a lot sooner than I will.

"Skintight is up every guy's alley," Courtney declared confidently. "What are you trying on?"

"Jeans," I said, pulling on a pair in my regular size.

"U.S. Girls jeans?" she asked, and I could tell she was laughing at me.

"So what? They're cute." And not only that, but my usual size was practically hanging on me. I just stood there, smiling into the three-way mirror.

"You're not still thinking about that stupid contest, I hope," Courtney said through my dressing room door.

"No," I lied. "I just need some jeans."

"Yeah, sure you do. Well, I'll be waiting outside whenever you get through fantasizing."

After she left, I tried on the next smaller pair, which were almost a little too tight. I had to fight to get the top button done, but when I looked in the mirror again it was worth it. My stomach is flatter than it's ever been, and I was right about that style showing it off. But then I realized that the contest is still four weeks away. So I not only bought the jeans, I bought them one size smaller yet. They're in my closet right now. And yes, I know the odds aren't in my favor, with girls trying out from fifty states. And getting my parents to let me drive a hundred miles to St. Louis is going to take some major begging. Not only that, but when Court finds out I'm entering, she'll make fun of me for hours.

Still, there's one important point I can't help thinking Courtney's missing. In clothes modeling, it's more important to be thin than beautiful.

And I'm getting very, <u>very</u> thin.

❊ ❊ ❊

Wednesday

Well, I'd barely gotten in the door from school today when Mom sprang big news—she wanted to take me and Heather shopping for shoes. There's a good news/bad news scenario if I've ever heard one. New shoes = good. Being seen in public with Heather = so bad. I thought about trying to whine out of it, but then I came to my senses. I mean, new shoes are going to last a lot longer than a shopping trip with Heather.

Of course Heather wanted to go to all those dorky athletic places. Running shoes are fine for kids like her, but I wanted platforms. Mom compromised by taking us to a department store where they sell both. Mom was in a pretty good mood today, actually. I don't know what came over her. Not that she's usually in a _bad_ mood, but she's definitely not the most patient person I know. Of course, raising Heather would try the patience of a saint.

"Those shoes are stupid," was the first thing Heather said when I finally found a pair I liked. She and Mom were sitting on one of those little benches, with shoes spread out everywhere, and I was checking my feet in the mirror.

"You'd be the expert on stupid," I told her. "Look what _you_ picked out."

"At least I'm not going to break a leg," she

said. She's such a baby. She still doesn't care how she looks at all.

"Girls, girls. Knock it off," Mom said. But it was one of those automatic kinds of comments, like she wasn't really paying attention.

"If I _do_ break a leg, at least it will be because of my shoes and not because I'm just an uncoordinated dweeb," I told Heather. I thought that was pretty funny, but I probably should have kept my mouth shut, because it brought Mom back to Earth.

"Those _are_ awfully high," she said, giving my new shoes a second look. "And I can tell you from experience, those soles won't flex at all. You really have to know what you're doing to walk in platforms. If you step on a rock or something and fall off the side—snap. There goes an ankle."

"_Everyone_ at my school wears them, and I don't know _anyone_ who's broken an ankle," I said, shooting Heather a dirty look.

"Well, neither do I," Mom admitted. "But that's what everyone says."

"I'll be really careful," I promised, imagining how great red platforms would look with my U.S. Girls jeans.

"All right," Mom said at last. "You're sixteen, and I guess that's old enough."

I smirked at Heather and Mom raised an

eyebrow at me, but by the time we got to the register she was lost in space again. The girl had to ask her every little thing, like, Are you paying by credit card, and Can I see some ID, and Do you want the receipt in the bag? Mom's usually all over that stuff. And normally she would have picked out some shoes for herself, too, but she didn't even look. I wonder what she was thinking about. What <u>could</u> she be thinking about? There's nothing in her life except us girls and Dad and the house.

I'll bet when she was my age, she never imagined her life would turn out so boring. I mean, she was Homecoming queen, and she still looks pretty good. I'll bet all the guys liked her. She probably dreamed about leaving Missouri, and having a successful, glamorous life somewhere else. I mean, who <u>doesn't</u> dream about that?

Dad, maybe. Dad's completely different from Mom. She still really cares how she looks, but he's just a regular guy, a little gray around the edges. I'll bet he was the one who wanted to stay here. I'll have to ask her sometime.

<u>I'm</u> getting out, though. There's no way I'm living in a small town all my life. <u>No</u> way. At least if I married Jesse he'd take me to California.

Not that I really believe that's going to

happen. I haven't completely lost my grip on reality. I'm still so mad at him! And the thing is, what makes me even madder is, I'd forgive him in a second if he even looked my way.

❀ ❀ ❀

Thursday

Well, you'll never believe what I just saw! U.S. Girls has a big ad about its modeling contest in this month's <u>Modern Girl</u> magazine! If the whole world didn't know about this thing before, they know about it now. It's weird to imagine girls all over the country opening the same magazine and seeing the same ad—like little Clearwater Crossing is finally connected to the rest of the world. In fact, this contest could be my ticket out of here!

I wonder if it will be like the Miss America pageant, with a tiara for the winner? I could get used to wearing a tiara, and carrying one of those enormous bouquets of red roses. What a thrill it would be to do that final victory walk down the runway, with everybody cheering. Wouldn't that be great? As soon as I finish writing this, I'm going to fill out my entry blank. I was reading it a minute ago, and it says they're going to pick one winner from every state. Then those fifty girls get to go to Hollywood for the finals in January. They'll pick five winners in that contest, and those girls will be the models for a national modeling campaign. Just reading about it got me so excited that I got my new jeans down out of the closet and tried to put them on.

Okay, so I wasn't so successful with that. I only bought them two days ago, so what did I expect? I didn't even try them on at the store, because I knew they wouldn't fit, but seeing that ad got me so fired up I decided to try it anyway. After all, I've lost fourteen pounds altogether, and I have hipbones and everything. I could barely get those pants pulled up to my waist, though, and forget about buttoning them. I had this whole big triangle of flab hanging out.

I have to admit I started to panic. I mean, there was no way those pants were closing. And they won't be closing next week, either, or even the week after that. But then I remembered that the contest is still four weeks away. I have _plenty_ of time to diet. I just have to be smart about this—I have to stop eating completely. Because I _have_ to win this contest. I've known that almost from the second I first saw that poster. This is my chance to fix everything! When I'm a famous model, my entire life will change for the better. Stupid Heather will show me some respect, Mom and Dad will have to give me more freedom and let me see the world, and at school I will <u>finally</u> be popular. Not just a little bit, oh-yeah-I-know-who-she-is popular, the way I am now. <u>Mega</u>-popular. Melanie Andrews popular.

And the best part of all will be the chance to laugh in Jesse's face. How I'll love paying him back for the way he treated me! I can just see myself sauntering past him in the quad with an adoring guy on either side of me and a whole gang following along behind. <u>Cute</u> guys. No, <u>college</u> guys. No, <u>fellow models!</u> Wouldn't that just serve him right?

When I get famous, I'm going to pretend I don't even know who Jesse Jones is.

✹ ✹ ✹

Friday

Well, we had another Eight Prime meeting at Peter's house last night. We were supposed to be figuring out what kind of fund-raiser to do next, but nobody seemed too into it. I know <u>I</u> wasn't but even Jenna seemed grumpy, and that's not like her at all.

"No more car washes," she said the second

Peter asked for ideas. "Let's do something else this time."

"Let's sell something," Jesse suggested. "That's easier than washing cars."

Jenna smiled at him, but I'm still not even looking his way if I can avoid it. I'm not looking at Melanie, either.

"What should we sell?" Ben asked.

Leah said that if it was later in the year, we could sell Christmas decorations, like wreaths.

"October is only a week away," Melanie-the-Genius informed us. "How about something for Halloween?"

"Like what?" I asked. "The only thing anyone buys for Halloween is candy, and since we can't get it cheaper than anyone else, how would we make a profit?" She thinks she's so smart, but she just shoots her mouth off like everyone else.

But then Peter had the idea of selling pumpkins.

"Pumpkins?" Jesse repeated. "Produce wasn't exactly what I had in mind."

"Think about it, Jesse," Peter insisted. "Nearly every family buys at least one to make a jack-o'-lantern. If we buy a lot of them, we might find a good deal at a farm somewhere. Then we could sell them at a profit."

"A <u>farm</u>?" Jesse said, like he'd never heard the word before.

"Welcome to Missouri, surfer dude," Melanie muttered under her breath. I don't know if she thought she was funny or what. How is Jesse supposed to know what kinds of stupid things we have around here? If I were lucky enough to be from California, I wouldn't care about farming either. I'm <u>not</u> from California and I <u>still</u> don't care about it.

"The Ozarks are practically famous for their pumpkin crop," Jenna told Jesse. "I think Peter has a good idea."

"Then let's sell them at school," said Melanie. "We could sell them in the quad during lunch."

"That would be fun!" Ben said.

"I don't <u>think</u> so!" I said. "Could you all maybe think of something <u>more</u> embarrassing to do?"

I mean, give me a break. It's one thing to do charity on the side, but I have enough problems already without being completely humiliated at school. Like I really need the entire student body to see me hanging out with Ben. Again. It was a pointless, <u>stupid</u> idea, and I especially don't want to do it with <u>her</u>.

"I agree with Nicole," Jesse said. "We don't need to do this at school."

It wasn't like he was supporting me—he just didn't want to do it either. Probably he doesn't want to be seen with <u>me</u>.

"I don't see what the big deal about selling pumpkins at school is," Miguel said. "I think we'll need permission, though. Probably from the principal."

So then Jesse got the bright idea that he and Melanie should be the ones to ask for permission, since they're so much greater than the rest of us mortals. "Principal Kelly will be more likely to let us hold the sale if we're the ones who ask him," he said.

But Melanie said she didn't <u>want</u> to ask. I don't know what her story was—it was her stupid idea in the first place. She probably just wanted to make him kiss her butt more.

"I'll ask Principal Kelly," Leah volunteered. "My parents know him, so it's no big deal. I'm sure he'll say yes."

"And maybe Jenna and I can start looking for a deal on pumpkins this weekend," Peter said. "We'll drive to a few farms and check out their prices."

So that was settled, that was <u>all</u> we got done, and I don't think I was the only one who couldn't wait to get out of there. I mean, when Kurt died we were all full of good intentions. But we don't really even know each other. Some of us don't even <u>like</u> each other. It's kind of a lot of pressure.

I wonder how much buses cost?

❁ ❁ ❁

Saturday

I <u>hate</u> myself! I can't believe I gained half a pound yesterday! I don't even know what I ate. It must be water. I'm <u>praying</u> it's water. How will I ever compete in the U.S. Girls contest if I turn back into my old disgusting self?

I just have to get serious about changing myself, that's all. And I mean <u>really</u> serious. I'm going to make a list <u>now</u>, while I'm still upset about this, so I won't have any excuse for forgetting later.

<u>Things I Have to Change About Myself:</u>
1. My weight! I'm the biggest, ugliest, most disgusting whale that ever walked on two legs.
2. The way I act. I <u>have</u> to be less shy around guys. I talk to them, but I act like such a dweeb!
3. My hair? I thought it looked pretty good a few weeks ago, but maybe it's time for a change. I wish Mom would let me dye it!

4. My attitude. They say people become what they believe. Which reminds me, I could pay more attention in church, too. I've really been meaning to do that.
5. My life. (That ought to cover everything else.)

Sunday

Well, I almost fell asleep in church again today. I really did mean to pay attention, but Pastor Ramsey could get a job as a hypnotist or something. The man just rambles. I tried to stay focused by staring at the Bible in my lap, but it was no use. The only way I could stay awake was to think about something else, and my favorite thing to think about lately is how devastated Jesse is going to be when I win that modeling contest. Won't I love rubbing his snobby, too-good nose in that!

I was so wrapped up in thinking about it that I almost missed the cue when everyone stood up to sing. It turned out I knew the hymn, though, so I was able to fake it. Dad kind of rumbled along like he always does, but Mom embarrassed me, as usual. If she wants to be an opera star, why doesn't she join the choir? I mean, that's what those people are up there for, right? They don't

<u>expect</u> the rest of us to sing much. Nothing against Mom, but it seems like showing off to me.

Of course as soon as I realized I was wishing I could melt through the floor, I had to ask myself if that wasn't pretty shallow of me, worrying about what people would think of my mom's singing. I mean, that's exactly the type of behavior I'm trying to outgrow. So why is it that when the embarrassing thing is happening I still act just the same? It's only afterward that I realize I've messed up.

Then I started to wonder if it's all this thinking about the modeling contest—and getting even with Jesse—that's getting me off track again. For a few hours, right after Kurt died, everything seemed so clear. It was like I suddenly realized that the road I was on wasn't going anywhere. I even thought I knew how to move in a different direction. But it didn't last. I still kind of remember what I was thinking, but it's already getting fuzzy. If I stray too far off my new road, I'm afraid I'll lose it altogether.

Which might be a good reason not to enter the U.S. Girls contest. But how can I pass up the chance to be what I've always dreamed—a real fashion model? And how can modeling be bad for me, as long as I keep my priorities straight?

So I've decided to go ahead and enter the contest. Now that I know what my goals are, I don't see any reason why I can't be a deeper person and a model too. Besides, aren't I working my butt off with Eight Prime? That's got to be earning me points somewhere.

❈ ❈ ❈

Monday

We had a "pumpkin progress" meeting behind the cafeteria today. Everyone in Eight Prime brought sack lunches to eat on the grass while Peter and Jenna briefed us about the pumpkin shopping they did over the weekend.

"There are two different farms I think would give us a good price," Peter told us. "And we'll get at least some pumpkins donated. But before we do any real negotiating, we need to decide how many pumpkins we think we can sell."

"Tell them about the church sale," Jenna said.

"Yeah, we need to talk about that, too," Peter told us. "I spoke to Reverend Thompson yesterday. If we want to, he'll let us sell pumpkins in our church parking lot one Sunday after services. I think we'd get a good response, because our congregation knows all about the Junior Explorers."

"It's a good idea," Melanie said. She always acts like she's in charge of speaking for the whole group. "Peter and I already discussed it in private."

"I think we ought to do it," Ben said. "If your congregation already supports the Junior Explorers, selling them pumpkins ought to be easy." He was eating tuna or something, and he had this huge glob of mayonnaise quivering on his upper lip. The guy is <u>hopeless</u>, I swear.

Peter nodded. "I think we'll do well, and so do my parents."

"Mine too," Jenna chimed in. "They've already promised to buy us girls a pumpkin apiece."

"That's a pretty good haul right there," Leah joked.

So we finally agreed to hold two sales: one at school and another at Peter's church.

"How many pumpkins do you guys think we'll sell?" Miguel asked Jenna. "And what are they going to cost us?"

Jenna said she thought they might sell a hundred at the church she and Peter go to. "A <u>hundred</u>?" Melanie said. "Just how big is this church?"

"Probably nearly every family there will buy at least one, and some will buy two or three,"

Peter said. "Look at the Conrads—they're buying five."

"I wonder if we can sell a hundred at school, too," Leah mused.

"At least!" Ben said. "We've got <u>fourteen</u> hundred students here."

"Yeah, but how many of them have any money?" I asked. I don't get any <u>joy</u> out of bringing these things up, but these people get so carried away. "And how many will spend it on a pumpkin if they do? That's the kind of thing your parents buy."

"We need to play up the charity aspect," Melanie said, like she's such an expert. "People will buy them if they know they're helping little kids."

"I'll bet we can sell more like two hundred at school," Jesse said. "Especially if we get the sports teams on board. I'll bring in the football players if Miguel will talk to the water polo team."

Miguel said he'd let the other players know.

"Well, then, are we willing to commit to three hundred—or as close to that number as we can afford?" Peter asked. By then I was tired of arguing, so I just went along with everyone else. I mean, you can lead a horse to sense, but you can't make it drink. Something like that.

"When are we going to hold the sales?" Melanie asked.

"First we need to make sure we have the pumpkins," Peter said. "And Leah still needs to talk to the principal. I don't think we're in a big hurry, though. It might be better to wait until later in the month."

"We shouldn't wait <u>too</u> long," Ben said. "Otherwise everyone will have already bought one."

The only good part about the whole meeting was when Peter decided we didn't need to meet again this week. We're supposed to get together after he and Jenna talk to the farmers he's picked.

I really don't know if I'm going to be able to stick this thing out. Eight Prime, I mean. I only agreed to do it under pressure, and I was so upset that day I barely even knew what I was saying. But now that I'm back to normal, I'm starting to realize what a huge mistake I made. Being forced to deal with Melanie and Jesse nearly every day really, <u>really</u> stinks. It's like I'll never be able to get over him, because he's always in my face. Not that I <u>want</u> to get over him. And that's why this group is so bad. I see him and I start going all mushy again, hoping for things that will never happen. And then he chases Melanie right in front of me. What I'm saying is, there are limits to what a person should be expected to put up with. I want to get the Junior Explorers a bus, but their summer camp only lasts two weeks and this sentence with Melanie is starting to look like two <u>years</u>.

All I'm saying is, I can't take it much longer. Something had better happen fast.

Tuesday

Well, I'm definitely competing in the U.S. Girls contest now, because I can't back out after what happened today. Courtney and I were eating lunch on our favorite bench in the quad— I should say <u>Courtney</u> was eating—when Jenna showed up with a brown bag in her hand and asked if she could join us. Of course I said yes, but I was surprised because lunch was already halfway over and Jenna always eats with Peter. At least I was on the ball enough to scoot closer to Court and make Jenna sit on my other side. Keeping those two apart is just common sense.

"I told Peter I had to study during lunch, but I finished early and now I don't know where he is," Jenna said. Then she pulled out a salami sandwich and started eating as if she hadn't touched food in days, which isn't too likely if you've ever seen her.

"So, what were you studying?" I asked, mostly to distract myself from my growling stomach. It was bad enough sitting and starving through Courtney's lunch.

"We had to memorize two new songs for choir," she said. "I had so much other homework last night that I didn't get around to it." And then she must have noticed my eyes glued to her sandwich. "Do you want a bite?" she offered. "I'll split it with you."

Of course I was embarrassed to have been so obvious, and it's not like there weren't other things I could have eaten—if I was eating. I didn't want to explain about the contest and my diet, though, so I told her I already ate.

"She did not," Courtney said right away. "Nicole doesn't eat anymore."

Sometimes Courtney drives me crazy. I know she was just paying me back for making her sit with a member of the God Squad. But what was I going to do after a crack like that? I had to admit I was on a diet.

"You? You're so thin!" Jenna said. "What do you need to diet for?"

It was a nice compliment, and I was about to

thank her for it, when Leah stepped out of the crowd and asked if she was missing something.

"No, just me wolfing down my lunch before class," Jenna told her. "Where's Miguel?"

"I don't know," Leah said. "Why would I?"

I was wondering the same thing, but Jenna just shrugged and returned to her sandwich.

Courtney scrunched over to make a place for Leah at her end of the bench. "Sit down," she said. "Nicole was just telling us about her anorexia."

This is my best friend, right?

"I am <u>not</u> anorexic!" I said. "Geez, Courtney. I'm just on a diet."

"I thought you'd been losing weight," Leah said, turning sideways on the bench to look me over. "You're thin enough now, though, aren't you?"

"I thought you were thin enough before!" Jenna said.

I was still irritated with Courtney, but I have to admit it felt good to finally have people notice. Of course, Jenna's opinion can't be taken seriously, because she could stand to lose a few herself. But Leah's extremely thin, so what she says means something.

"I'm getting there," I said. "I still have another few pounds to go, though."

Leah raised her eyebrows. "I think you're there," she said firmly. "You don't need to lose any more."

I don't know why, but I started getting really embarrassed. I think it was because they were all staring at me. "Thanks," I muttered. "But they say the camera adds ten pounds, so models actually need to be underweight in order to look good in pictures."

"You're a _model_?" Jenna asked.

"Every night from midnight until two A.M.," Courtney snorted. "Or whenever it is that she dreams."

"Funny, Courtney," I shot back. I was so annoyed I didn't even stop to think what I was saying. "For your information, I've decided to compete in that U.S. Girls contest."

That dropped her jaw. She looked absolutely stunned. "I thought I talked you out of that!" she said.

"Not arguing with someone isn't the same as agreeing with them," I told her. "Believe it or not, I don't do everything you say."

Court was obviously getting ready with some sort of sarcastic comeback when Leah asked what the U.S. Girls contest was. I took a few deep breaths, and then I told her all about the store's new line of jeans and how I'd be going to St. Louis to compete in the Missouri portion of the contest.

"Wow!" Jenna said. "That sounds exciting."

"Did your parents say you could drive to St. Louis?" Courtney asked at the exact same time. She just can't _stand_ it when I do something she isn't part of. She always has to be in charge.

"It _is_ going to be exciting," I told Jenna. "You ought to come." The invitation was out of my mouth before I even knew it was coming, but Jenna looked so thrilled I didn't regret it a bit.

"You mean, go with you?" she asked excitedly. "Oh, that would be so fun! Peter never wants to do things like that."

"We all ought to go," said Leah. "Let's invite Melanie, too, and make a day of it."

"What a _good idea_!" Courtney said, jumping on that train as fast as she could. "That would be _great_!" Of course she knew that was the last thing in the world I wanted, short of cancer or something. I could have kicked her for agreeing to such a horrible plan. She was still just getting me back for having a thought of my own.

"Well, _we_ can all go. But I don't think there's going to be room in the car for Melanie," I lied. "Not unless _you_ want to stay home, Court," I added, but Courtney only laughed.

"Are you kidding?" she cackled. "I wouldn't miss this trip for anything."

Sometimes I wonder why Courtney and I are still together. I mean, we've been best friends forever, and I really do love her. I can't even imagine life without her. But lately it doesn't feel like she's on my side very often. I honestly think she only wants to go to St. Louis so she can make more fun of me if I fail. And that's just not right.

I'll bet Jenna would never do that to Peter.

Wednesday

Well, I've decided that Courtney did me a favor. If it weren't for her, I might have chickened out on the U.S. Girls contest, but now I can't. Whatever Court's motives were, that's a good thing.

It's funny, but it's always been kind of that way with us. When I'm around her, I'm just braver. Or maybe she just knows how to push me into things better than anyone else. Either way, we're like a team.

I still remember the first time I saw her, the day she transferred into Mrs. Kinderling's class. Fourth grade! She hadn't figured out how to control her curls yet, and it looked like her hair was exploding or something. The color was so bright then too. Now it's clearly red, but back then it was closer to orange. She stuck out worse than a cat at a dog show, and I was practically the only person who wasn't whispering about her behind her back. I couldn't. I didn't have anyone to whisper to.

I wasn't exactly the most popular kid on the playground. I don't know why. I mean, there wasn't anything <u>wrong</u> with me. I was just easy to pick on for some reason. The first day Courtney came, I was sitting under a tree at the edge of the pavement, just trying to keep a low profile, when she walked right up to me.

"You're in my class, right?" she said. "What are you doing over here when everyone else is over there?"

I still remember exactly how she looked when she turned to point to our playing classmates. Even then, she knew how to dress. She was wearing this cute flowered shirt and low-hanging jeans that were worn out in all the right places. Just a sliver of belly showed when she twisted around to point, but still—provocative by fourth-grade standards.

"I know how to make French braids," I blurted out.

After that, we just got kind of inseparable. And pretty soon Courtney got such a reputation for her quick comebacks that no one dared say anything mean about her, even when we <u>didn't</u> braid her hair. Better still, they didn't dare say anything mean about me. We were a unit, and everyone knew it. I wouldn't say Court <u>rescued</u> me, but she did kind of give me a reason to finish elementary school.

By the time we hit junior high, people had forgotten all about the fact that maybe I wasn't quite as cool as I could have been back in fourth grade. Courtney and I were practically famous for our fashion sense by then. And we were tight, about as tight as two people can be. (Until that Emily Dooley thing, but I don't feel like going into that right now.) What I'm trying to say is that Courtney and I have a history. We've been through a lot together. And even though lately it feels like she's gone off the bossy, sarcastic deep end, she's still my best friend. She's the best friend I've ever had.

Well! That was mushy! I don't even remember how I got off on that subject. Oh, yeah. Because Courtney bossed me into the U.S. Girls contest. Or maybe it was more like she <u>reverse</u> bossed me into it. Either way, I'm in it now. I really ought to thank her. Especially since Melanie's not coming. What a nightmare that would have been!

I can just see Melanie getting to St. Louis and

all of a sudden deciding to compete in the contest. Why not? She competes with me in everything else. She would probably beat me too. I mean, I'm not ugly. I can mostly hold my own. But next to her I <u>feel</u> ugly. We both have blond hair, but hers turns heads even when she lets it hang, and I really have to work on mine. We both dress nice, but her clothes are five times more expensive than anything in my closet. One thing I have is good eyes—that same bright blue as Mom's. Melanie's are a pale, washed-out green, but there's something about them that pulls you in anyway. Plus everything she does is just so confident. The way she walks, even the way she <u>stands</u>. I don't think she's ever had an insecure moment in her life. At our school, she's like the queen of the world. I honestly think you could fill our cafeteria full of supermodels, and if Melanie Andrews walked through all the guys would look at Melanie. I don't know what it is about her. I mean, I kind of do. I see it too. But I can't describe it any better. She's just practically a different species.

At least she's short. I probably have four inches on her, and for modeling it wouldn't hurt if I was even taller. Leah is the perfect height. I'd guess she's about 5'10", which is plenty tall enough to model and still short enough to find guys who are taller. I wish I was 5'10". Jesse's probably about 6', so it would work out perfectly. Except that I'd have to wear flats all the time, and that would get old fast.

I wonder if Leah's ever considered modeling? It doesn't seem very likely. She's so studious, and even though she dresses all right she doesn't pay <u>that</u> much attention to her clothes. If she'd let me make her over, though, I'll bet she'd be really pretty. She has kind of an exotic thing going already, with her olive skin and hazel eyes. The right eye makeup could really play that up. She's probably not interested, though, and I don't think I have to worry about Jenna jumping into the contest. Not that she isn't pretty. Jenna has the most flawless skin I've ever seen, and really long, thick hair. But she never wears a bit of makeup, and I hate to say it but she needs to lose some weight. Not that she's huge, but if I were her I'd want fifteen pounds off <u>now</u>. Maybe she could cut back on those cookies she's always eating.

Ha! Another "C" food! I'm going to put this away and start writing out that diet now. This could make me really rich!

❁ ❁ ❁

Thursday

Well, this time Courtney really messed up. At lunch today I asked her what time I should pick her up for tomorrow's football game and she said she was going with Jeff. With <u>Jeff</u>! And if that wasn't bad enough, she acted like it was <u>my</u> fault for not making some sort of appointment with her earlier. Give me a break! We <u>always</u> go to home games together. We've been to every single one since freshman year!

I really yelled at her, not even caring that we were in the middle of the quad. "You know I don't have anyone to go with now," I said. "How could you do this to me the day before the game? Now I'm going to miss seeing—"

I was too upset to even finish the sentence, but we both knew what I meant. <u>Not</u> that I care about seeing Jesse play—it's the principle of the thing. Anyway, I made a pretty big scene, for me. I think I embarrassed her.

"I'm sorry, all right?" she said. "Do you think you could calm down now?" That's about as close to apologizing as Courtney ever comes, so she must have known she blew it. "Why don't you go with someone else?" she asked. "Maybe you can hook up with the God Squad."

I just gave her a dirty look. After what she'd

just done, I couldn't believe she'd dare to call them that.

"Er, I mean Jenna and Peter," she said, amazingly catching the hint. "They're probably going."

"They probably are, but I can't ask them _now_," I said. "I'll look too pathetic."

"Oh, please," Courtney scoffed. "They're not going to care."

Doesn't she get it? _I_ care. She tried to tell me I was making a big deal about nothing, but the two bites of sandwich I'd let myself eat felt like two bricks in my stomach. Worse, I knew I was going to start crying. I mumbled something, threw my food away, and took off.

The thing is, it's not just that I think I'll _look_ pathetic, I _am_ pathetic. Courtney can't imagine how it feels to be the only one without a boyfriend, without a date, without even a _girlfriend_ to hang out with. I feel like a total reject. And I don't care how mad I am at Jesse— the thought of missing this game is so depressing I can barely stand it. I _never_ miss a game.

I _have_ to win that modeling contest. If I'm ever going to be anyone at this stupid school, that's the only chance I have. Maybe if I'd made it onto the cheerleading squad, then modeling wouldn't be so important. But I'm so lame I couldn't even make the cut. Meanwhile, Melanie Andrews becomes the first sophomore cheerleader in the history of Clearwater Crossing. I know I shouldn't hate people, but it's hard not to hate her.

She gets <u>everything</u> I want.

Friday

Well, this has got to be the worst night of my life. I can't believe I'm missing the game. At least Mom let me drive her car today, so I was able to go to the video store after school. I got that new Ethan Ryan romance—the one Courtney's been dying to see—and I'm going to watch the entire thing without her. If I'm lucky, I'll be able to spoil the ending for her later. It's the least I can do, after all she's done for me.

I was reading this article in <u>New Look</u>, and it said that if your friends don't treat you right, it's because you let them. Supposedly something <u>I'm</u> doing is telling Courtney to treat me the way she does. Personally, I think that's all wrong. For one thing, that author's never <u>met</u> Courtney. If she did, she'd probably have to revise her whole theory. I liked my horoscope better, so I cut it out and I'm pasting it here.

> An unfortunate alignment of the planets
> has been making your life feel like uphill
> work. But never fear—your turn to shine
> is on its way! Don't be afraid to try new
> things, make new friends, and go new
> places. Success is sure to follow!

Isn't that perfect? It's like my life <u>exactly</u>. Trying new things must mean I should be in the modeling contest, making new friends is kind of what I'm doing already with Eight Prime, and the new place must be St. Louis! Plus, it says success is sure to follow. That's probably the best horoscope I ever got. Usually they're just kind of stupid, like they're so vague that they could mean anything.

　　Well, I'd better get going because Mom's going to call us for dinner any minute. I figure if I stick mostly to salad, I can sneak a cup of air-popped popcorn during the movie.

Saturday afternoon
　　Well, I just got off the phone with Jenna, and it's nice to know I'm not the only one with sister problems. The main reason I called her was to find out about the game last night. I saw her and

Peter at the last one, so I figured she was probably there and wouldn't mind being pumped for a few details. I could have called Courtney, but I'm still kind of mad at her, and the last thing I wanted was to subject myself to a bunch of Jeff stories. Knowing Courtney, she'd probably say something stupid like they didn't see the game because they were making out in the bleachers the entire time. She loves to lie about stuff like that, because she knows it embarrasses me. I've told her a hundred times that I'm not a prude or anything, but still, there are limits.

Anyway, I called Jenna with some excuse about the pumpkin sale, then asked if she'd gone to the game. She and Peter were there, and she said she saw Leah and Miguel up in the stands, but she hadn't spotted Ben. Like I care! I didn't even think to ask her if she'd seen Courtney because what I really wanted to hear about was Jesse. Unfortunately, Jenna seemed more interested in Melanie.

"You should have seen her!" she said. "The cheerleaders have a new stunt where Melanie does a flip off one of those little trampolines and lands on top of the spirit pyramid. It looks really hard and scary, and everyone went crazy cheering for her."

"Really?" I said. She was totally rubbing salt in my wounds, but I couldn't tell her that. I mean, Jenna obviously <u>likes</u> Melanie.

"Oh, yeah," Jenna said. "Even though she's the youngest, she's probably the best cheerleader on the squad. Maybe she'll be captain next year."

Wouldn't that be great? All we need is for that girl's head to get any bigger. Not to mention that I'm still hoping to make the squad next year myself.

"So did Jesse play much?" I asked. I already knew the Wildcats had won, because I heard the final score on the radio.

"Yes. Well. Not quite as much as last time," she said.

Jenna is <u>so</u> nice. I could tell she was trying to put things in the best possible light, but it turns out our football hero wasn't too on his game last night—a couple of missed patterns, a couple of dropped balls, and a general lack of impressiveness. That must have <u>killed</u> him after he had the whole stands screaming for him at the season opener. Hearing that should have cheered me up a lot, but I'm such a dope that I actually felt kind of sorry for him. I just couldn't help thinking that if things were different I could have been there for him, to make him feel better after the game. I would know exactly the right thing to say, or I'd have a special little inside joke or something, and Jesse would say how he can never be sad when he's around me. That would be so great—if it wasn't a complete fantasy. Anyway, I suppose he had Melanie there for that.

We were pretty much done talking about the game when all of a sudden Jenna asked me to hang on a minute and I started hearing all these weird noises. It sounded like she had a hand over the mouthpiece and there was a bunch of yelling going on in the background. I couldn't figure out what the deal was until Jenna came back on.

"That was Maggie wanting to use the phone," she said. "She only wants to use it because I'm on it now. No one touched it for two hours before you called, and she didn't need to use it then."

"Well, I'll let you go," I said.

"No way! Don't hang up!" she told me. "Now I have to stay on twice as long, just to teach her a lesson."

Of course that made me laugh, because I knew exactly what she was talking about. Sharing a phone with Heather is no joy either. I told Jenna all about what a pain she is—barging into my room at all hours, making snide remarks every chance she gets. I left out the part about her sick crush on her Sunday-school teacher because I wasn't sure how Jenna would take it. I mean, we both go to church, but I have a feeling Jenna gets a lot more out of it than I do. I didn't want to offend her.

"That's nothing," Jenna said. "Barging into your room? I <u>share</u> a room with Maggie. I never get away from her! And if you could see how our room looks now, you'd vomit."

Maybe, but I was laughing like crazy by the time Jenna finished telling me about the war the two of them have been having the last couple of weeks. It started with Maggie leaving her dirty clothes all over their room. Jenna asked her to stop but she wouldn't, so Jenna finally hung Maggie's new pink bra and panties from a nail outside their second-story window. No one could see them from inside, but anyone in the backyard would have a perfect view. A day later, Maggie realized they were missing and got in a total panic, thinking she'd lost them in gym or something. Jenna finally told her where they were, then said she'd seen this guy Maggie has a crush on riding his bike past their house and pretended maybe he saw them from the sidewalk. Maggie was screaming! I was laughing so hard I was tempted to do the same thing to Heather, just for the heck of it.

But unlike baby Heather, who would just run

crying to Mom, Maggie got even. The next day, when Jenna came home from school, half her room had been wallpapered with posters for this band called Clue that Maggie likes and Jenna hates. They sound really putrid—the posters, I mean—purple and orange and fluorescent green. And the way Jenna tells it, Maggie used a ruler to make sure she covered every centimeter of her side and not a millimeter of Jenna's. She even did her half of the ceiling! And since all the posters are completely on Maggie's side, there's not a thing Jenna can do.

Which didn't stop her from trying. She got a couple of spare sheets and pinned them up like a room divider so she didn't have to see Maggie. But the next day, when she came home from school, her mom had taken them down and she was in trouble. Not only that, but somehow Maggie managed to turn it all around with their parents so it looked like everything that had happened was Jenna's fault. Jenna got yelled at, and Maggie got permission to go to the Fall Fantasy—that <u>stupid</u> junior-high dance—with the same bike-riding guy she's crushing on.

So of course Jenna wanted nothing to do with her a few days later when Maggie started acting all buddy-buddy. They got into a big argument about how lame the Fall Fantasy is and Maggie got offended and stormed out. Jenna thought she'd finally gotten the upper hand, but I'll tell you what: Maggie is dangerous. She's twice as scary as Heather—even on Heather's <u>best</u> day. I'm almost afraid to write what she did next in case Heather ever sneaks a look at this and gets any ideas.

Maggie took a picture of Jenna when she was sleeping, with her mouth wide open and some goofy nightgown on, and posted it on the Internet! Right in the CCHS guest book. I never log on to that, but Jenna said people were staring at her all the next day and she couldn't figure out why. She ended up finding the photo herself, completely by accident. Maggie had put a caption under it that said, "Hi, I'm Jenna Conrad. I'm a junior and I think I'm great!" Or something like that. The kid's some sort of evil genius.

Well, Jenna got Maggie grounded, so she's not too happy with Jenna. If I were Jenna, I'd actually be kind of scared right now—although it's hard to imagine how Maggie could top the Internet stunt. Jenna doesn't seem too worried, though, and they've both taken their lumps. Maybe Maggie's had enough. Still, after everything

Jenna told me, I think Maggie's the type who'd have to get the last word. She reminds me a lot of Courtney, actually. It's kind of scary to think what they could accomplish if Maggie and <u>Courtney</u> were sisters!

Sunday

   I lost a pound! I rule!!!

   I'd write more, but we're on our way to church and I don't have anything new to say anyway. Except that I really <u>am</u> going to pay attention today—no matter <u>how</u> boring the sermon is!

Monday night, late

   Well, I never thought I'd be this worried about Melanie Andrews, but I really, really am. All of us in Eight Prime spent the whole afternoon at the hospital, but she still hasn't regained consciousness and now they're not going to let anyone see her until tomorrow. If she lives that long. I actually feel kind of sick. I mean, I've never pretended to like the girl, but I don't want her to <u>die</u>.

   It all happened today at lunch. The cheerleaders were doing some kind of pep thing in the quad to celebrate Friday's win. Courtney was nowhere to be found, so I was hanging out on my own. So many people were there watching that you couldn't really tell who was standing with who anyway. Lou Anne Simmons brought a boom box, and Vanessa Winters walked around clearing people out of a circle of concrete near the center of the quad. As soon as they had enough room, the whole squad did a dance there. Then Vanessa made some sort of speech about our 2-and-0 season and the girls started forming the spirit pyramid. That was when I first spotted the mini-tramp and realized they were going to do that new flip thing Jenna had told me about. Melanie backed way up to get a big run at it.

The thing was, I couldn't believe they were doing the stunt on concrete. I'm not even on the squad and that was the first thing I thought of. At the time, I was even kind of disgusted, like Melanie thinks she's so great it wouldn't <u>occur</u> to her that she could fall. But of course that's exactly what happened. As far as I can tell, she was supposed to jump off the trampoline, turn a full flip in the air, and land standing on the backs of the top two girls in the pyramid. Jenna said it came out perfect Friday night. But Melanie's timing was off today. She opened out of her flip too soon, and instead of landing on Tiffany and Cindy, her feet kind of skidded along their backs. She tried to catch her balance, but everything happened so fast that she fell backward off the top. Even with all the noise and confusion, I heard her skull hit the concrete. I think everybody did.

Peter was the first to react—he was screaming her name even before she hit the ground. I saw him running toward where she'd gone down, but then the crowd closed in and everyone started pushing. I couldn't get to where they were. Then a bunch of teachers showed up. Everyone was yelling and shouting directions at each other. It was really chaotic and really horrible because Melanie never got up. She never even <u>woke</u> up. They drove an ambulance right into the middle of the quad, and somehow Peter convinced Principal Kelly to let him ride to the hospital with her. Once the ambulance pulled out, the crowd started to move again, and I was finally able to get to Jenna. We wanted to go to the hospital too, but neither of us had driven to school so we didn't have a car there. Then somehow Jesse and Ben found us and we all went straight to the hospital in Jesse's BMW.

I thought Jesse was going to kill us, the crazy way he was driving. Jenna even told him to slow down. When we got there, Melanie was still unconscious, still in Emergency, and Peter was in the lobby. Jesse was freaking out. He wanted to force his way in to see her, but Peter talked him out of it. "You're going to get us thrown out of here," he said. "And even if they let you in, what good can you do her right now?"

He was right, of course, and Jesse finally settled down. Writing about this now, it seems like I should have been jealous, but at the time that never even occurred to me. I mean, things were just too serious. Anyway, we were sitting there waiting, hoping Melanie's doctor might come out and tell us some good news, when the lobby doors opened again and a man hurried toward the reception desk.

"I'm Clay Andrews," he said, in this low, nervous voice. "My daughter's school called and said there'd been an accident. Melanie Andrews— how is she?"

The receptionist had barely given us kids the time of day, but she snapped to attention when she heard that. "Oh, Mr. Andrews! Dr. Levenstein wants to see you right away. Follow me, please."

She led him down a corridor while we all stared after him, amazed. I don't think any of us expected someone so fabulous to have a father who looked like <u>that</u>. He's on the short side, a little stooped over, and his <u>clothes</u>! They looked like they came right out of a laundry hamper. My mom would <u>never</u> let my father dress that way.

"Did you see that?" Jesse asked as soon as he was out of earshot. "Did you see Melanie's dad?"

"He's not exactly the way I pictured him," Ben said, apparently opting for understatement.

"To say the least!" Jesse said. "All I can say is, she must take after her mother."

"Give him a break," Peter told them. "Imagine how worried he must be."

"We're <u>all</u> worried," Jenna said. "I wish they'd tell us if she's okay."

About an hour after we got there, Leah and Miguel showed up. They'd gone off campus for lunch and so they didn't hear the news until they were already in fifth period. It didn't really matter, though, because we still didn't know anything they didn't. Finally, around dinnertime, the receptionist told us to go home. She gave us a number we can call to see if there's any change in Melanie's condition, but I've already called it a couple of times and they keep saying she's still unconscious. I guess I might as well go to bed, but I have a feeling I won't sleep much.

It's weird, but I think I'll really be sorry now if anything happens to her. Anything permanent, I mean. I'd be lying if I said she's my favorite member of Eight Prime, but she _is_ a member. And Eight is the key word here. We started with eight, we should finish with eight.

I really _do_ hope she's okay.

Property of

Melanie Andrews

Room 243

TUESDAY

There is nothing to do in the hospital except watch soaps and dwell on the past. Since neither thing appeals to me and it looks like I'll be stuck here awhile, I thought I'd start a sort of diary. Actually, I'm writing this on a blank artist's pad, but the paper doesn't matter, right? It's the thoughts that count (ha ha). I don't know, maybe any diary I would write is only a different form of dwelling on the past, but anything's better than just lying here. And _maybe_ something new will happen that I can write about—although I doubt it. Now that it looks like I'm not going to die, the excitement is probably over.

It feels strange to think that for a while I honestly didn't care if I lived or not, but that's the truth. Or maybe the real truth is that I was actually kind of hoping I'd die. If death is as peaceful as being unconscious, then I don't see how it can be bad. I don't know. This whole experience is probably the weirdest thing that's ever happened to me. When I was younger, I was terrified of dying. I've been over that a long time, but I never thought I _wanted_ to die before— which is kind of astonishing, now that I'm thinking about it. It was just the most amazing feeling when I was drifting in and out of consciousness, like I was floating in warm water and everything was very, very safe. My head didn't hurt a bit. (It hurts _now_ — I thought that nurse was bringing me some aspirin.) The whole time I had the weirdest sensation, like someone who cared was watching over me. Even in those flashes where I half realized I'd been hurt, and that maybe I wasn't going to wake up again, I wasn't scared at all. I couldn't say why. It was kind of like being little again, and not being afraid of the dark because you know your parents are right in the next room.

Eight Prime stopped by a little while ago, and I found out Peter rode here in the ambulance with me. He was the first one to get through the crowd when I fell, so the medics let him come along. Now that I'm thinking about it, though, he must have pushed his way through all the cheerleaders — they had to be closer to me than Peter. I'm surprised Vanessa didn't come, since she's the captain.

Surprised, but glad, I have to admit. I don't think Vanessa likes me that much, although I can't think of a single thing I ever did to her. Maybe I'm just imagining it. On the other hand, she _did_ make me work with Jesse at the carnival, even after I told her I don't like him. She practically called me chicken to goad me into learning that stupid stunt. But the best evidence is just the way she looks at me — like seeing my face really ruins her day. I don't know. Maybe it does.

Well, I really wanted to write more about Eight Prime's visit, but I'm so tired all of a sudden I can't keep my eyes open. I'll have to get back to this after I take a nap. I'm not worried. I'm afraid there'll be <u>plenty</u> of time.

* * *

TUESDAY NIGHT

It's a good thing I caught a nap earlier, because I don't think I'm going to get any sleep tonight. There are so many strange noises here, and people in and out of my room every five minutes. Dad went to a lot of trouble to get me a private room, but it still feels like I'm sleeping in the middle of a McDonald's. It's the total opposite of our house, where only two people live in that whole giant space — not to mention that our concrete walls suck up sound like a vacuum. I never hear <u>anything</u> there. I've been trying to fall asleep for the last hour, but now I'm just giving up.

It's strange but suddenly I'm not that tired

anyway. I guess I was just kind of hoping that if I fell asleep I might see Mom again. I still don't know what to make of seeing her before, leaning over my bed like that when I first woke up from the accident. I was still half out of it — I was probably hallucinating. But it felt so real. I mean, literally. I didn't just see her, I felt her hand stroke my forehead. It gives me goose bumps just remembering. I wish I could talk to someone about it, but who would I tell? Not Dad, that's for sure. So far this accident has scared him sober, but if anything would send him running for the bottle again, that would have to be it. He can still barely stand to talk about Mom, and besides, he doesn't believe in an afterlife. I don't believe in an afterlife. It's a nice fantasy. But it would have to be a whole lot better than this life before I'd want to sign up. Eternity is way too long to put up with half the stuff that happens here.

Oh well. Since I can't sleep, I might as well write about Eight Prime. I wanted to do that before, so I guess this is my chance. It was strange to see them all here in my hospital room today. It was even stranger that they all came. I mean, I know Nicole doesn't like me because of what happened between her and Jesse (I'm not saying it makes sense). And speaking of the devil, if I hadn't been so mad at Jesse, I probably never would have fallen in the first place. On top of that, I was really worried that Peter or Jenna was going to say something religious in front of my dad, and my head still hurts too much to hear all his reasons God doesn't exist. Again. Besides, I know them by heart.

Nothing bad happened, though. Dad's actually being pretty cute, like he suddenly thinks he's my protector or something, worrying over every little thing. It makes me wonder how he thinks I got through the last two years without him, but I guess I shouldn't complain. Being babied is better than being ignored. When Eight Prime showed up this afternoon, I don't think he even wanted to let them in, like I was too fragile or something. Maybe I should have let him send them away, as awful as I must look, but I have to admit I was curious. It wouldn't have shocked me too much if one or two of them had shown up, but a visit from the entire group was a pretty big surprise. Besides, I wanted to find out what had happened after I passed out, and what people at school were saying about me. I hate being talked about behind my back.

I don't think I fully realized how close I had come to dying (or at least how close <u>they</u>

thought I had come) until I saw their faces. They all came filing in as if they expected to find a corpse. My head was still throbbing, and I could barely sit up, but I really wanted to talk to them. Dad took charge like the executive he used to be, moving the two chairs around and telling everyone else where to stand. I really wish he hadn't retired after Mom died. I know we don't need the money, but working would at least give him less time to drink.

By the time Dad got done rearranging everyone, all the guys were standing by the bed, and Leah had to sit by my feet because Jenna and Nicole had the only chairs. Jesse skulked behind Peter and Miguel, his eyes on the floor like I wasn't even there. I guess I can't blame him. After I slapped him Friday night, then told him to leave me alone on Monday, I have to give him credit for showing up at all. It was actually pretty embarrassing, facing him again, and I did wish I had been a little less nasty when he tried to apologize to me on Monday. But getting slapped Friday was his own fault completely. I'll <u>never</u> be sorry for that.

Then Peter gave me a bunch of flowers everyone had pitched in on, and Dad took off to find a vase. I think we all relaxed to see him go —

especially me. He was sober today, but he's so out of it most of the time that he doesn't even know who my friends are anymore. I knew he had no idea who Eight Prime was — to him they were just seven random people from my school.

"So how are you?" Jenna asked as soon as Dad left. "We've all been so worried about you!"

I told them I was fine, that I just split the skin on the back of my head and bruised things pretty good. I was still unconscious when they sewed me up, so I didn't even feel that part. "I guess they had to shave part of my head to do it, though," I added. "My dad says it's barely noticeable, but I haven't felt brave enough to look."

Leave it to Ben Pipkin. "I'll look!" he shouts, lunging right for my aching head. Somehow his foot caught Nicole's chair leg, and he ended up doing a full faceplant in the blankets over my kneecaps. The impact made me see stars. I was still gasping and Ben couldn't even struggle to his feet before Jesse yelled at him and pulled him backward off the bed by his belt, giving him a wedgie at the same time. Of course Ben was really embarrassed. Ben's _always_ embarrassed. I don't know how the poor guy gets through a day. Then Jesse called him "genius" and Ben turned even redder, apologizing like crazy.

"That's okay. You didn't hurt me," I lied to make him feel better. I don't know, the guy's a total klutz. He's _more_ than a klutz—he's a menace. But there's something about those wounded puppy-dog eyes of his that always makes me forgive him.

"I was only trying to help," he told everyone. "I was going to check Melanie's bald spot for her." Like I wanted him to.

Amazingly, out of all of them, Nicole was the one who got it. "If _she_ doesn't want to see it, she definitely doesn't want _you_ to, Ben," she said. "Figure it out."

And then my dad walked back in with a vase he'd borrowed from the nurses. All I can say is, it's a good thing he didn't see Ben's swan dive or he probably would have thrown everybody out. Since he didn't, though, and since suddenly nobody knew what to say, I felt like I had to introduce them.

"These are the friends I made at Kurt Englbehrt's carnival," I told Dad, hoping he wouldn't do his usual drinker's amnesia thing and ask, "What carnival?" I was really expecting one of those blank stares, but instead he actually seemed to remember who Kurt was.

"That was a good thing you all tried to do," he said. "Tragic, the way it came out." His voice kind of cracked a little, though, and I knew thinking about Kurt's car accident had made him think about Mom's. I started introducing everyone individually, to get his mind off that, but as soon as my dad heard Peter's name, he got distracted again.

"Peter Altmann?" he repeated, staring at Peter. "You're the one who rode with my daughter in the ambulance?"

Peter nodded, and that was how I found out about that, because I still don't remember anything between the moment I first realized I was going to fall and the start of those weird, half-waking flashes.

"The school told me how you refused to leave her side," my dad said to Peter. "I appreciate that. You're a good friend."

"It was nothing," Peter mumbled. "Any of us would have done the same. I was just the only one who could get through the crowd."

"I don't think it's nothing," Dad said, but he let it drop, since Peter was turning bright pink. "When Melanie feels better, you'll all have to come over to the house. We'll grill up some burgers and have a pool party or something."

"It's getting kind of late in the year for a pool party," I protested, but Dad only grinned.

"So we'll crank up the heater," he said. "If I

have to, I'll get one of those big white wedding tents put over the whole deck."

Ben got totally excited, but personally I wasn't sure what was more frightening—the idea of clumsy Ben by a body of water, or Ben's <u>body</u> by the water, in a bathing suit. It did sound fun, though, and everyone else seemed to think so too. I have to admit I'd forgotten how cool and generous Dad can be. It would be great to have him stay like this, but I'm not going to count on it. Sober wears off faster than alcohol with him, and I'm sick of getting my hopes up for nothing.

Well, I guess I'm pretty tired now. I'm going to try sleeping again, anyway. The sooner I get better, the sooner I can get out of this place.

* * *

WEDNESDAY

My head feels better today, but the rest of me feels worse. I must have bruised my entire back side when I fell onto the pavement. Lying here in bed so long probably isn't helping, but I don't have a lot of options. I can get up and walk to the bathroom, but that's about as far as I go before things start spinning enough to make me glad to crawl back into bed. I'm just going to have to sleep this off, I guess, but I wish I could do it at home, where I might actually <u>get</u> some sleep.

I wonder what I'm missing at school. Probably nothing. And I know I'm not missing anything at home. So why do I feel so restless? I feel like I'm missing <u>something</u>, even though there's nothing to miss. Except Mom, maybe. I still miss her every day. And seeing that vision or hallucination or whatever it was stirred up all these old memories until I can barely think about anything else.

Everything was different when Mom was alive. Dad was different, I was different—we were just a normal family. The last thing I'd call myself now is normal. I don't even know how to describe it, but now it's almost like "Melanie Andrews" is just a name that everyone knows instead of a real person. I'm a myth. Which is good, I guess, because if I had to be a real person now I'm not sure who I would be. I'm not even sure it would matter, since everyone else thinks they already know.

Everything was simpler when I was little. At least the people who hung around me then actually liked me for me and not because they thought I might rub off on them somehow. The girls did anyway. Guys have always only liked me for the way I look. I couldn't say that anywhere but here, where I know no one will see it, because it would be too easy for people to get the wrong idea, like I'm conceited or something. I know I'm not conceited—I barely even like myself. Maybe someone who's never been used by a guy could believe that having them constantly chasing you is a good thing. It's not.

I wish I could talk to Mom about guys. She was way prettier than I am—she'd know how it is. Maybe she could even give me some advice, but it seems like she died right when I needed her most. We got to do all of the kid stuff together, but who's going to teach me how to be an adult? I feel like I really got cheated, especially since Dad's made so little effort to fill her shoes. I don't expect miracles—I know he can't be my mother. But is it too much to hope for a father? He's not the only one who's hurting, and it makes me so mad sometimes the way he acts like he lost more than I did.

Well, the phone just rang and it was Tanya, calling to warn me that the cheerleaders are on their way over to surprise me. She wanted to let me know, in case I wasn't feeling up to the visit. I'm going to put this away now because I want to fix myself up and try to brush my hair before they get here. Eight Prime might forgive me for looking awful, but Tiffany will probably bring a camera and start shooting pictures for the yearbook. I don't know what's wrong with that girl. I don't even know why she's coming, but I really have to go.

* * *

WEDNESDAY NIGHT

Being in the hospital is really getting old. If it wasn't for writing this stuff down, I think I'd go crazy. The only other time the boredom is relieved is when someone comes in here to poke at me. It wasn't so bad yesterday, but I still don't understand why they couldn't discharge me today. I guess the thing about head injuries is that sometimes problems show up later. They <u>have</u> to let me go home tomorrow, though, or I'll really make a scene. Enough already.

The cheerleading squad was by here earlier. Dad had gone home for a while (lucky him!), so he missed them. They brought me a huge green-and-gold balloon bouquet, which they tied to the foot of the bed, and Angela tried to pretend that I look fine. She must think we don't have mirrors here. Thanks to Tanya I did look better than when Eight Prime dropped in on me, though. I still have a bandage on the back of my head, but a nurse helped me comb around it, and we even took a peek underneath. Dad's right. Once the stitches come out and they let me wash my hair and comb it right, that shaved spot won't even show.

"This is a heck of a way to get out of a few days of classes," Tanya teased me. "You just about gave us all a heart attack. Come to think of it, I'm actually kind of surprised Ms. Carson isn't here in the hospital with you."

"She telephoned earlier, and sent me some flowers," I told them. "She sounded pretty upset."

I think she feels guilty about the accident, since she's supposed to be our advisor and she wasn't even there. It was only ever a part-time job for her, though—she's really a language teacher. Everyone knows Vanessa runs things. Or she used to, anyway. As soon as I said Ms. Carson was upset, I could tell by the girls' reactions that something was going on.

"In fact, Ms. Carson said she didn't even know we were doing that spirit rally on Monday," I added, trying to find out what they were hiding. "She said she'd never have allowed us to do that stunt on concrete if she had."

Everyone looked at Vanessa. "I don't have time to tell her every little thing!" Vanessa complained, getting all huffy. "I only thought of it Sunday night, and I already had to call all of you. I had no idea she'd care."

"I doubt she would have," Tiffany said, "if she hadn't gotten in trouble. If Melanie hadn't fallen, everything would be fine."

"Well, excuse me!" I said. I can still barely turn my head without it throbbing, so the last thing I needed was to be accused of hurting someone else. To be perfectly honest, I didn't really need to see Tiffany today either. She only came for appearances' sake. Which is probably the same reason Lou Anne, and Sue, and probably Cindy came too, now that I'm thinking about it.

Tanya stuck up for me, though, like she always does. "Don't be silly," she told Tiffany with an annoyed look. "We're just happy Melanie's okay."

"Of course!" Angela echoed. Those two girls are my favorites by far.

"But we aren't allowed to do the new stunt anymore," Lou Anne said. "Principal Kelly put his foot down. We can still do the spirit pyramid, but not with the flip."

"_And_ we're getting a new advisor," Cindy said. "Someone who'll actually come to our practices and plan our events and everything."

"Who?" I asked.

"I don't know," Vanessa answered. She didn't let it show in her face, but I could tell from her voice that she's not happy about that _at_ _all_. Which is what I would have expected, considering how bossy she is. The last thing Vanessa wants is to have to deal with someone who outranks her.

"Whoever it is is bound to be an improvement," Tanya said. "They could grab someone off the street and do better than Ms. Carson."

"Maybe we'll even get to go to cheerleading camp next summer!" Angela said.

"Don't get your hopes up," Vanessa said nastily, and I just had to smile. If we do go, Vanessa won't be with us, because she, Cindy, Sue, and Tiffany are all graduating this year. What a shame. (I'm _kidding_!)

After the squad left, I had to admit that cheerleading isn't turning out to be as fun as I thought it would. I like the actual cheering, and the stunts are my favorite part, so I'm not just bumming because I split my head open. I mean, obviously I'm not thrilled about that, but—I don't know. I guess I just thought we'd be more of a team. Like we'd all be really close. It sure isn't that way so far.

Or maybe I'm just depressed about the Eight Prime pumpkin sale. After the girls left, Peter came by and I found out I'm going to miss it. We had planned to hold the sale later in the month, but now Principal Kelly is saying it has to be Friday and that's only two days away. There's no way I'll be back at school that soon. I think Peter knew I'd be disappointed, so he wanted to tell me himself, to cushion the blow a little. And I _am_ disappointed. More than I'd have expected. Not only about missing the sale at school, but even about missing the follow-up sale at his church this Sunday—which is weird, because I wasn't too wild about that idea at first. But once I made up my mind to do it, I started getting curious. After all, how many chances do I get to peek inside churches? And now I'm going to miss the whole thing.

"I'm so sorry, Melanie," he said. "I wish you could be there."

"Yeah, well," I said, not wanting to seem immature. "We don't always get what we want in this world."

"Just one more reason to look forward to the next one," he told me with a wink.

I was really tired by then and my head felt like it was caught in a vise, but I had to smile anyway. I mean, you would too, if you knew Peter. He's like that. He doesn't push, but he doesn't give up. I've met other Christians who were either always trying to convert me or else just informed me I'm going to hell and walked away to leave me to it. But Peter and I have actual conversations about religion. He knows I don't believe in God. I don't even believe it's possible for someone like me to change their mind about that. But Peter still insists that changing my mind is <u>all</u> I have to do. He makes it sound so simple, and it probably does seem simple — to him. Sometimes I think things must be so easy for people like Peter and Jenna, going through life with this perfectly mapped-out belief system and all those people there to support them. But it's definitely more than that with Peter. I mean, he's not just paying God lip service. I can tell he truly believes what he's saying. And it's funny, but knowing how sincere he is somehow makes it okay. I can listen to things from him I couldn't sit still for from anyone else.

Like when he told me he'd been praying for me. A few weeks ago, a comment like that would have made me squirm. (It still would if my dad was in the room.) But I'd have been surprised if Peter <u>wasn't</u> praying for me, so when he said that, I only smiled. "I hope it does me some good," I teased.

"You're still with us, aren't you?" he asked, smiling back.

"Yeah, about that," I said. "Why couldn't you have prayed I'd wake up in Hawaii, or someplace good?"

"Very funny," he said, but he knew I was joking. And the fact that he can <u>take</u> a joke is part of why I like him so much.

"You know, Peter, I've been thinking," I told him. "I don't remember you being with me when I was unconscious, but I think I must have known you were there."

"What makes you say that?" he asked.

"I don't know. It's just a feeling I had. I knew someone was with me."

"Well, I don't see why your subconscious couldn't have known," he said. "I was talking to you. And holding your hand."

"Really?" I didn't intend to embarrass him, but he turned scarlet. I wasn't saying it <u>meant</u> anything—it was just weird to think we'd been holding hands and I hadn't even known it.

"Well, yeah," he said. "I was terrified. When we got to Emergency and they made me go sit in the lobby, I thought I'd go crazy with worry."

That totally wrecked my theory, because if he went to the lobby right after we hit Emergency, then he couldn't have spent much time with me at all. And that feeling I had, the one that someone was with me, definitely hadn't ended after the ambulance ride. I had become so sure the someone was Peter! I wanted to ask him more questions, but I didn't even know what to ask.

After he left, though, I kept thinking about that, and about seeing my mother. Could there really be another world, something after death? Before this accident happened, I'd have said no for sure. And I'd still say no if I was in court or something. But I have to admit, I'm thinking about it now.

It's practically all I'm thinking about.

* * *

THURSDAY

Hurray! I'm finally home! It'll still be a while before I go back to school, but it's so nice just to be out of the hospital! And it's not like I'm desperate about missing classes. I'm sure all my teachers will be more than happy to load me up with whatever I'm missing when I get back. I'm still just lying around (unfortunately) but being in my own bed feels so much better. Maybe later I'll play some CDs or watch a video. Right now I just want to appreciate the fact that there are no phones ringing, no footsteps in the hall, and best of all, no one in sight but me.

Dad insisted on making me an omelet and bringing it up earlier, but I tried to have a serious conversation with him and he ended up running out of here. He's probably on his third or fourth beer by now. It seems like that's what always happens. This time he started out trying to tell me he loves me, and somehow that turned into how he blames himself for Mom's car accident—which is a stretch, considering he wasn't even there when it happened. It's not a stretch for Dad, though. Not at all.

Oh well. I guess I knew all this sobriety couldn't last. I mean, I hoped it would. I always hope it will. The thing is, I know Dad really _does_ love me, so why can't he just stop drinking? This is all so different from the way he used to be. He never used to drink when Mom was alive. Not more than anyone else, anyway. He had a job then. He had a _life_. Mom would be horrified if she could see what he's become. In fact, if Mom were here right now, I'll bet she'd kick his butt.

God, I wish she were here.

* * *

I'm missing the school pumpkin sale today.
I really wanted to help with that, but I still get
headaches just walking around. It would be fun
to see all the pumpkins piled up in the quad,
though, and the looks on everyone's faces. I've
always loved Halloween. It's the only day of the
year you can be anything you want.

I wonder if Jesse's bossing everyone around,
like he did at the carnival. I wouldn't put it past
him, even though selling pumpkins was Peter's
idea. Jesse always has to make himself look big,
no matter what he's doing. I think that's why he
loves football. He didn't look too big last week,
though. I wonder if he started drinking before
the game, because that would explain a lot.
He was sure plenty drunk afterward, when
he grabbed me outside the gym and tried to
make me kiss him. Just remembering turns my
stomach—all that liquor on his breath and the
smug look on his face.

And it's not like that was the first liquor he's
ever touched. Being drunk was his excuse for
using Nicole at that party and then throwing
her away like an old Kleenex. I have to admit I
was pretty irritated when Courtney said Nicole
blamed _me_ for that. He didn't do it because of
me—he did it because he has a drinking

problem. That's so obvious to me now that I can't believe I didn't see it before. I, of all people, ought to know the signs. And I do feel sort of sorry for Nicole now. She likes to pretend she's so cool, but I have a feeling she's actually pretty sheltered. She probably still has no idea what a bullet she dodged not getting involved with him.

All I can say is, Jesse had better watch where he's going. He ought to come take a peek at my father sometime, passed out surrounded by empties. I'm not claiming I'm perfect—I drank for a while after Mom died. I did a lot of things I'm not proud of. But you have to be pretty stupid to be in the middle of that mess and keep believing you're making things better. Drinking only makes them worse.

* * *

SATURDAY

Peter Altmann came over today. I was reading on a lounge chair out back and I never heard him knock, so I could barely believe my eyes when Dad showed him through the back door. What a relief he wasn't wearing that ratty old bathrobe! Peter brought me some of his mother's cookies and the cutest Get Well card that Amy Robbins painted at Junior Explorers. Here's what it says:

Dear Melliny,
I'm sorry you broke yore head. Dont
be sick any more. OK?

Love, Amy

Isn't that adorable? I like her so much. Maybe
it's because both our mothers died, and that
gives us something in common. Or maybe it's
just because she's really, really cute.

"The kid has a way with words," I joked, not
wanting Peter to know I had a lump in my throat
the size of a fist.

"She was pretty upset when she found out
you'd been in the hospital all week and no one
had told her," Peter said. "She thought Chris
and I should have brought the Junior Explorers
there to see you."

Can you imagine? Sixteen rambunctious little
kids crammed into that closet they had me in at
the hospital? My head hurts just thinking about
it. I like the Explorers a lot, but I'd rather see
them at the park when I'm feeling better.

Peter told me that Jenna and her sisters are
trading bedrooms today, and that's why she
didn't come with him. Actually, I was glad to see
him alone. I really like Jenna. But I like Peter
more. There's just something about him that

makes me feel like things are all right—and I don't feel that way very often. Besides, I wanted to talk to him about that weird thing that happened with my mother, and I could never mention that if anyone else was around.

"You know what we talked about at the hospital?" I said. "About how I thought maybe I knew you were with me, even though I was unconscious? Well, it wasn't just in the ambulance."

"What do you mean?" he asked.

"I don't even know exactly how to explain it," I said. "It's just that the whole time I was passed out, I felt like somebody was with me, like I wasn't alone anymore. I mean, not that I'm <u>alone</u>. But this was different."

"Uh-huh." He had this ridiculous grin on his face and I could tell he'd already decided that I'd had some sort of close encounter with God. That was all right. I knew he was going to.

"At first I thought it must have been you," I went on. "Then you told me they separated us at the emergency room. But there had to be doctors around the whole time. Later, my dad came. So then I thought it <u>wasn't</u> you—that it was a bunch of different people."

"Uh-huh," he repeated, still grinning. I had to look away to keep from smiling myself.

"The thing is," I said, "that doesn't make sense either. It was one person with me from the moment I blacked out till the moment I woke up. I know it was. I felt it."

"But you've already ruled out all the possibilities," Peter said, finishing my thought. "You know there wasn't any one person around the whole time."

"Right," I agreed. Our eyes locked, and I noticed he wasn't smiling anymore.

"So who do you think it was?" he asked.

"I don't know," I admitted. Then I finally managed to spit out the big question. "Do you think it could have been my mother? I mean, I _saw_ her, Peter. At my bedside. I opened my eyes and there she was."

"You were dreaming," he said softly.

"It didn't feel that way," I said. "It didn't feel that way at all."

"You already know who I think it was," Peter said. "Your mother may have been watching, but I don't think she's the one you felt beside you."

"Then why did I see her?" I asked.

"I don't know," he admitted. "Maybe because you felt the type of love you used to get from her. Is that what it felt like? Love, I mean."

I got excited for a second, because it _had_ felt

like love. But then Peter took it too far. "Or maybe it was an angel," he said.

It was all I could do not to laugh. I mean, I was glad he was taking me seriously, that at least he believed I'd seen <u>something</u>. But an angel? Extremely unlikely. If such things even exist, I doubt they'd bother with me.

"I thought angels weren't supposed to look human," I said. "Isn't that what it says in the Bible?" Not that I'm an expert. I've never even read the Bible. But you hear things. You pick stuff up.

"They can take human form," Peter said. "Perhaps, if one wanted to comfort you, then—"

"Then you think it could have looked like my mother?" I said.

"Maybe. Or maybe you just thought it did. I'm not saying it <u>was</u> an angel, Melanie. I'm just saying search your heart. Be open to the possibility. You already know that I think God was with you the whole time. I think you felt his presence. But he could have sent an angel."

"You really believe that, don't you?" I asked. But it was a rhetorical question—I already knew he did. And then I remembered something else I've been thinking about a lot. "You know how you said people can change their minds about

God? Do you think that really happens? I mean, <u>really</u>?"

"I think it happens every day."

"Why?" I asked.

"Because I think he calls people," Peter said without hesitation. "He calls people and they feel it. Maybe they don't know that's what's happening—maybe they don't want to <u>believe</u> that's what's happening—but they come to him just the same."

I don't know. That sounds pretty far-fetched to me. But sometimes I feel like there's this big aching hole inside me, and I have no idea how to fill it. The next thing I knew I was blurting out that maybe I'd come to his church sometime. Of course he jumped on that. He wanted me to go tomorrow morning, and even offered to come pick me up. I had to backpedal like crazy. I don't even know why I said that, except that I feel so confused this week.

I guess I <u>did</u> hit my head pretty hard.

* * *

SUNDAY

Once there was a princess who lived in a big concrete castle. She had everything money could buy: a suite with a view, a closet full of clothes, a swimming pool, a housekeeper. She had everything money attracts: admiration, status, popularity. And she had none of the things her heart desired.

The princess hid in her castle with those thick walls around her, practicing the smile she wore anytime she stepped into the world. Every day she practiced, making it a little wider and a little brighter, refusing to acknowledge the sadness in her own eyes. Because the princess had one thing she valued above all the rest: pride. Whenever she left her castle, it was with her head held high and that smile on her lips. And the smile fooled the people, and no one ever guessed that their princess was really a peasant after all.

Okay, so I'm bored. And feeling sorry for myself because I'm missing the last pumpkin sale. But that's just what's wrong with me <u>today</u>.

Everyone thinks that being Melanie Andrews must be so great. Well, let me tell you—it's not. Not even close.

If they ever make a movie of my life, they ought to call it <u>When Reality Attacks</u>.

* * *

MONDAY

I saw Dr. Levenstein this morning. He says I can't go back to school for a couple more days (I can't believe I actually want to) and that even when I do there won't be any cheerleading for a couple of weeks. Not even practices. I can't wait to hear what Vanessa is going to say about that! At least he took my stitches out and I finally got to wash my hair. That little patch he shaved is already getting stubbly, and it doesn't show at all unless you go looking for it.

After the excitement of a shower, though, I was out of things to do again. I finally decided to paint something, just to pass the time. Dad was downstairs fooling around in his office, so it seemed like as good a time as any to sneak into Mom's studio. He's never said I can't go in there, but he and I both avoid the place—out of respect, I guess. I've hardly been in there at all since she died.

I don't know what I expected when I opened the door, but I didn't expect it to be so sunny. I guess part of me wants it dark now that she's gone, but Mom never had any blinds put on those huge windows so it's practically the brightest place in the whole house. At first I was just thinking I'd grab what I wanted and take it somewhere else. When I was a kid I needed Mom's permission to go in her studio, and being there without her still feels like intruding. But then I realized how much easier it would be to paint with those big easels over a floor I didn't have to worry about dripping on. Plus all the paint and canvases and paper are in there, and I didn't even know exactly what I wanted to use. I ended up deciding to stay and do a watercolor. Watercolors were always Mom's favorite—we have hers hanging all over the house—and I got kind of nostalgic remembering her teaching me to paint them.

She wouldn't have been too impressed with my first attempts, though. I hadn't painted in so long that I was totally out of practice. But eventually I got the hang of it again and I ended up painting a landscape for Peter. It's no big deal—I just wanted to do something nice for him, because he's been so nice to me. And it came out pretty well, if I do say so myself. It's all these dark clouds over an empty field, with light breaking in everywhere. I hope he likes it. I may have mixed feelings about the rest of Eight Prime, but I'm really glad I met Peter.

I just had a scary flash—could I be starting to fall for this guy? I'd better not, because that would just be crazy. I don't have much use for guys to begin with—not after Jack Bailey— but Peter and I as a couple are practically unimaginable. There probably aren't two more different people in all of Clearwater Crossing. I definitely like him. I like him a lot. But the two of us together would be a total freak of nature. You know what, though? Now that I'm thinking about it, the <u>perfect</u> couple would be Peter and Jenna. It's weird that they've been friends all these years and never figured it out.

Oh well. Just painting a guy a picture doesn't mean anything. Still, I can't wait to see his face when I give it to him. Maybe I'll call and find out if he can come over tomorrow.

* * *

TUESDAY

Peter and Jenna stopped by after school today and I gave Peter his picture. I think he really liked it. I'd meant to have it framed and ready before he got here, but I was still fooling around with the bow when they came up to my room. At least I was dressed in regular clothes, looking more or less back to normal. The thing I hated most about being hurt was looking so pathetic. I can deal with looking bad, but I really hate looking helpless.

Jenna seemed amazed when she realized I'd painted the picture myself. She said she thought I'd bought a print, which made me feel pretty good. I'm not nearly the painter Mom was, but the compliment was still nice. I told Peter he should hang it in his room, and I think he will. But then I noticed the way Jenna was gawking at my room and I started getting really uncomfortable. She acted like she'd never seen a walk-in closet or a private bathroom before. I know I have a nice room—I didn't invite them up to show off. The fact is that it's embarrassing to have people make a big deal about the house. I finally got them down to the sitting room by pretending I wanted a soda. As soon as we left my room, though, Jenna got awfully quiet, and I didn't know what to think. I started worrying that Peter had made her come, or that I'd offended her or something.

"I'm going back to school tomorrow," I told them. "You won't have to make any more sympathy calls on poor little me."

"Like we minded!" Peter said. "We've all been really worried about you. Haven't we, Jenna?"

"We have," Jenna said. So then I felt all right again, and I asked Peter to tell me about the pumpkin sale at their church. They sold nearly all the pumpkins, which is good because I guess things didn't go as well at school as we thought they would. There are only a few little pumpkins left over, and Peter is going to let the Junior Explorers decorate those for their next project. Some of the kids were there helping on Sunday, so I guess they're pretty excited about that. I wish I could have seen Amy surrounded by all those pumpkins, but the main thing is, we're one step closer to the bus.

There's an Eight Prime meeting at Jenna's house Thursday night, and Peter will have a treasury report by then, showing exactly how much money was raised. I should be able to go to the meeting if I don't get too tired at school. And since I'm not allowed to do any cheerleading, I can't imagine how I'd get tired.

It's going to be weird to be back at school, though. It's just over a week, but it feels like a lifetime has passed since I hit my head. Like I'm a completely different person now. That doesn't make any sense, I know. Oh well. I know what I mean.

* * *

WEDNESDAY

I am _so_ tired! I have the worst headache, and I'm not even going to _look_ at any more homework tonight. Forget it. I'll just have more to make up later. I can't even remember now why I was in such a hurry to go back to school. Boredom is better than torture. You should have heard Tiffany at lunch. Not, I'm glad to see you. Not, How do you feel? Not Tiffany.

"I thought they shaved part of your head!" she complained, like I'd really let her down by not showing up half bald. "You can't even see it!"

"They did a good job," I said.

"You look great," Tanya told me to smooth things over. "No one would even know."

"No one would know <u>except</u> that you're missing the game this Friday," Vanessa said. "I don't know what we're going to do about that." I'd actually expected her to be kind of mad, but she was surprisingly human about it. And I just about fell off my seat when she asked me if I thought the squad ought to deal with my absence by leaving a gap or by reassigning positions to fill the hole. I couldn't believe that <u>Vanessa</u> was asking <u>me</u>. She even wants me to dress and come sit on the bench on Friday, so everyone can see I'm all right. Maybe she likes me after all.

I was kind of hoping Peter would walk by our table and tell me how my painting looks in his room, but I didn't see him—he and Jenna were probably eating outside. The only other Eight Primer I saw was Jesse, lurking by the cafeteria door. I have no idea what he was doing, and I don't care. As far as I'm concerned, he and I are even now. I'm not mad at him anymore — I just don't want anything to do with him. I made sure none of the other cheerleaders even saw me glancing his way, because they all used to think I had some sort of thing for him. Ha! He had some sort of thing for <u>me</u>, and even that is over now. I assume it is, anyway. It had better be, because it is never, ever going to happen.

<u>Why I'll Never Go Out with Jesse Jones</u>
He's conceited.
He drinks.
He only wants me to make himself look good.
He was a total slime to Nicole.
He's the type who would kiss and tell.
He's the type who would change his mind.
✱ I don't need the aggravation!!

Oh, yeah! I almost forgot. I ran into Leah and Miguel in the library after school, and they're a couple! I caught them fooling around behind the book stacks and there was no way they could deny it, although they obviously wanted to. I'm the very first person to find out. No one else in Eight Prime even knows. Leah swore me to secrecy, though, so of course I had to promise I wouldn't tell. I'm not sure exactly <u>why</u> it's such a secret, but it is more romantic that way.

I'm happy for them. They look really cute together.

* * *

THURSDAY

We had an Eight Prime meeting at Jenna's house tonight. We got a lot done, but I'm starting to wonder if I'm ever going to be completely normal again. Between school and that long meeting, I feel like I just finished a marathon (not that I could <u>ever</u> run that far).

Jenna showed us girls her new room before the meeting. If I have the story straight, she used to share with a younger sister, but then her older sister moved in with her youngest sister and now Jenna has a room to herself. Something like that—all those sisters get pretty confusing. Anyway, she's up on the third floor now, and she seems pretty happy about it. Personally, it's hard for me to even imagine sharing a room with someone. It's not that I wouldn't want to so much as I just can't imagine it. Leah's an only child too, so I wonder if she was thinking the same thing.

As soon as we got back downstairs, the guys told us Ben had another fund-raising idea, which turned out to be a haunted house. Peter had figured a profit of $1,128 on the pumpkin sale (pretty good!) and Ben thought that since Halloween was working for us we ought to stick with it.

"There was this Christian college group that used to do a huge haunted house in my neighborhood," Jesse said, with a big, nostalgic smile. "You should have heard the rumors that went around school every year before it opened — they made you put your hand in cow guts, they made you sit on a bench that gave electric shocks, there was a crazy guy with an ax pretending that he worked there. By the time my friends and I finally got inside, they could have shown us Bambi and we'd have been terrified."

"Did they really give people shocks?" Ben asked with his eyes bugging out.

"Of course not. Are you kidding?" Jesse answered. "They'd have been sued blue. No, it was just a bunch of kids with overactive imaginations. It was a blast." Then he sighed, like he really misses the old days. I wonder if he hates Missouri as much as he says, or if it's just that he misses California.

"It does sound kind of fun," Jenna said.

"It does. But I'm not sure it's feasible," Leah put in. "I mean, for one thing, where would we hold it? We can't exactly have it in someone's garage."

There was a long silence while everyone thought that over.

"That _is_ a problem," Jesse finally admitted. "That haunted house I was talking about, they used to do it in an enormous abandoned building. And it made a pretty big mess, too — what with paint and fake blood and kids wetting their pants everywhere."

"Gross!" squealed Nicole. "Jesse!"

You heard it here first — I don't think Nicole's given up on Jesse. She got him to drive her to the meeting, and she was so pleased with herself that she was practically having giggle fits all night. I don't know what she thinks has changed. Any objective person can see he still isn't into her. Oh well. If she likes to learn things the hard way, I'm sure Jesse will accommodate her.

"We'd need a bunch of props, too," Leah said. "Even if we had a building, we'd have to build a ton of scary sets. We'd have to wire in sound effects, and spooky lighting. Then there's costumes, tickets, advertising. No way could we do something like that with only eight people. Not only that, but we'd have to manage the line, sell tickets, guide kids through, act like spooks inside . . ." She trailed off as if completely overwhelmed, and when I thought about what she'd just said, the project did seem pretty impossible.

"I guess it's not such a good idea," Ben said, looking crushed.

"No, it is," Miguel said. "It just might be too big for us."

"It would cost a lot to buy all that stuff," I said. "If we didn't get a good turnout, we could lose all the money we've made so far." I felt sorry for Ben, but somebody needed to point that out.

"Oh, no. We're not buying everything," Peter said decisively. "But what if we could get most of it for free?"

And then he explained what he had in mind. "The building's still a problem, but let's forget that for a minute," he said. "What if we asked the CCHS drama department to help with the props and costumes? When they find out the bus we're buying is to honor Kurt, they might lend us a bunch of stuff. We might even get some volunteers that way. I know my parents would chaperone and take tickets—we could <u>all</u> ask our parents to help. And don't forget about Chris and Maura and their college friends. Between them and us, we ought to know plenty of people."

"He's making it sound almost doable," Jesse said. Personally, I think Jesse wanted to do it more than any of us—even Ben.

"We'd still have to buy some stuff," Peter admitted, "but probably not that much. And if we advertise, and run the haunted house three or four nights in a row—"

"I'll bet we could get five dollars a ticket," Ben piped up.

"Five dollars?" Jenna said. "Do you really think so?"

I told her the big ones in St. Louis get more like ten. I know those are professional, but ours is for charity, and that ought to count for something.

Jenna started doing the math. "If we got a couple hundred people a night, at five dollars a head," she said, carried away by the idea, "that would be—"

"A lot of money," Nicole said. "A whole lot more than we've made so far. I think we ought to do it."

"Maybe we <u>are</u> ready for something a little

bigger," Leah said. It's hard to argue with $5 x 200 people x 3 or 4 nights.

"But what about the building?" Miguel asked. That pretty much shut us down. By then everyone wanted to do it, and Peter's ideas had solved a lot of problems, but there was no getting around the fact that we didn't have a place.

"There's got to be somewhere," Jenna said finally. "Maybe someone's parents know of a building we can use. If not, we could ask around at church this Sunday."

"I think it's worth a try," Peter said. "We should at least ask before we give up."

So we just kind of left it on the table. If we can find a place, we'll go for it. Otherwise, it's back to the drawing board. Personally, I'm kind of hoping a place will turn up. I think it would be a lot of fun.

* * *

FRIDAY

I'm killing a few minutes before Tanya picks me up for the game tonight. I'm not going to cheer, but I am going to sit with the squad. When they're sitting, that is, which probably won't be too often. I'll probably be alone on the bench 90 percent of the time. If I had a choice, I'd rather sit in the stands, or even stay home, but Vanessa made such a point of including me that I really don't have a choice.

Oh well. Tomorrow ought to be fun. A while ago Jenna called and asked me if I wanted to take her place on a one-day trip to St. Louis. I'm still finding this hard to believe, but apparently Nicole's in some sort of national modeling contest??? Leah and Courtney are going too, but Jenna can't now, and since I'm up and around again she thought I might want to. I'm a little leery about the fact that Nicole didn't invite me herself, but I probably wasn't well enough when they made their plans. At least she seems to finally be off her high horse about me, and Leah and Courtney are pretty cool. Besides, I'm sick of being cooped up indoors. It will be fun to go on a long car ride, just four girls on the loose. Plus the Skyline Mall is huge. Maybe I'll do some shopping.

Well, I'm going downstairs now to make sure I'm out the front door the second Tanya's car pulls up. Dad's been drinking, and I don't want him playing greeter. Especially not in that ratty old bathrobe.

* * *

MORE FRIDAY

I guess I finally got caught up on my sleep, because I woke up two hours ago and I've been tossing and turning ever since. And I just realized that even though I wrote up there that it's still Friday, it's technically Saturday now. If I don't get back to sleep, I'm going to be useless tomorrow. I mean today. In a few hours I have to get up for that St. Louis thing.

I shouldn't have gone to the football game. It's not like I care whether we win or lose. I <u>pretend</u> to care. I have to—I'm a cheerleader. But I don't. Not really. And I don't care how much Jesse plays or how well he plays in the slightest. It's just that tonight he played really awful—and I can't help wondering if he's okay. I mean, he's already proven that his coping mechanisms aren't too stellar.

I don't know what was wrong with him tonight. He was dropping passes and running around like he didn't know what an end zone was. People were booing him, and shouting mean things. Maybe he couldn't hear them out on the field, but I could hear every crack from the cheerleaders' bench. The thing is, he started out fine. He even made a few good plays. But then he dropped a pass, and after that he just fell apart. It was like he couldn't believe he'd made a mistake, and he couldn't get over it, either. He didn't even seem sure why he was out there. I really thought Jesse was far too vain to ever look so pathetic in public.

The dropped passes were nothing, though, compared to that one spectacular fumble. Hank was about to be sacked so he fired off a wild Hail Mary. No one was expected to catch it, but Jesse came streaking out of nowhere. He raced down the field and amazed everyone by actually snagging the ball. The whole crowd was screaming for him—until he fumbled. Then the nearest Mustang picked up the football and turned it over for the touchdown. It's ironic, but the Wildcats would have been better off if Jesse had let that pass drop.

And if that wasn't bad enough, Coach Davis benched him after that. Jesse sank onto the wood with his head in his hands, like he was trying to hide from the world. Maybe it wasn't the smartest thing to do, especially since a little humility couldn't hurt him, but seeing him so low made me feel like cheering him up. We hadn't even talked since the accident—and I'm embarrassed to say this, but I was starting to miss him a little. I wish we'd never had that stupid fight. At the time, though, I was just so sick of him following me around, trying to score, and it didn't help that most of the school seemed to think we were a couple. I just wanted to put some distance between us. I still do. Just maybe not quite so much.

So when Coach Davis went down the sideline to yell at somebody else, I ran over to Jesse's bench. I told him to cheer up, that things weren't that bad, but he just looked at me as if I'd crawled out from under a rock.

"What are you doing here?" he said sullenly. "I thought you were mad at me."

"I guess I got over it," I said.

"You sure have lousy timing," he told me. "Everyone else is just getting into it."

I really can't stand self-pity. Besides, it wasn't even true. He has one bad game and he turns it into the whole school hates him?

"Oh, please," I said. "So it's not your night. Big deal. We're still going to win, and you'll play better next time."

"They won't even let me on the field next time. This is it. I'm finished," he said, like Mr. Drama. Still, at least we were talking again, and even though he wasn't looking at me, I got the feeling he was glad I'd come over.

"Don't be ridiculous," I said. "You're practically their star player."

"Are you making fun of me?" he demanded.

I was about to tell him I wasn't, when all of a sudden Coach Davis started yelling right behind me. "This isn't a coffee klatch, ladies!" he screamed, all teed off. "We're supposed to be playing football, not exchanging gossip!"

He scared me so much that I practically flew back to the cheerleaders' bench. I didn't even say good-bye. Jesse just groaned and dropped his head into his hands again. I felt terrible. I <u>still</u> feel terrible. I mean, I was trying to make things better and instead I got him in trouble with the coach. I never even saw him after the game to apologize. I hung around awhile, thinking that he'd show up, but he must have gone to The Danger Zone because I missed him somehow.

I wonder if he's mad at me?

I couldn't really blame him if he was. Except that I didn't have anything to do with the way he <u>played</u>. And the Wildcats did ultimately win. It would be kind of nice if Jesse and I could put the past behind us and be friends now. Nothing romantic — that's the last thing I want. But if he wants to call a truce, so do I. After all, as much as we're going to see of each other in Eight

Prime, it would be a lot easier to like him than hate him.

Unless, of course, he hates me.

I should have just stayed on my bench!

* * *

SATURDAY

Well, this has been the weirdest day ever. Nicole picked me up at dawn (at least that's what it felt like) for the big trip to St. Louis. Leah and Courtney were already in the car, and Courtney had a box of donuts for everyone. The rest of us pigged out, but Nicole wouldn't touch one bite. She said she ate at home, but I could hear her stomach growling from all the way in the backseat. Courtney started teasing her about how much she's been dieting, and that's when I realized that she <u>has</u> lost weight since the beginning of the year. I didn't know her last year, but Courtney said she lost weight over the summer, too. I don't know how much thinner she wants to be — she looks all right to me.

The mall was completely mobbed. Girls were packed in everywhere, and it seemed like most of them were there for the U.S. Girls contest. Nicole almost fainted when she saw the competition. I honestly think that was the first moment she fully realized what she'd gotten herself into.

"I tried to warn you this was a national contest," Courtney said, obviously enjoying Nicole's state of panic. "Of course, this is only the Missouri turnout. In some of the other <u>forty-nine</u> states, they probably got even <u>more</u> contestants. Don't worry, though, Nicole. I know they're only picking one girl here, but when you get to the finals in California, they're taking a whole big five."

"I feel sick," Nicole gasped. She <u>looked</u> sick.

Leah laughed and leaned over the second-story railing. There was a whole sea of girls down below us. "If you aim right, you could knock out quite a bit of the competition that way," she said.

The four of us took an escalator down to where everyone was standing in line to register. I could tell Nicole was still really nervous — more nervous, probably. And then, when we finally got to the front, the lady behind the desk thought <u>Leah</u> was there to enter the contest. Leah couldn't have been less interested — she wasn't even dressed up. But the registrar lady twisted her arm, and then Nicole <u>really</u> twisted her arm. Personally, I think she was just afraid to go backstage by herself and she wanted Leah to hang out with. Leah finally agreed, just to make Nicole happy, and Courtney and I found seats out in front of the stage and runway that U.S. Girls had rigged for the girls to compete on.

Their folding chairs were incredibly hard, but at first I didn't mind. At least the mall was a change of scenery. The contest took forever to get started, though. Then, once it did, it took even longer to get to Nicole and Leah. They had this really lame music blaring, and one by one the girls walked out to the end of the runway, posed, turned, and walked back again. They only got about twenty or thirty seconds each, but there were over 300 of them before Nicole.

"Now I know what they mean by a cattle call," I told Courtney. "This thing is endless."

"You're not kidding!" Courtney said. "I don't even know how they're going to pick someone. Everyone's starting to look the same."

Which was the complete truth. U.S. Girls had made this dumb rule that all the contestants had to dress in red, white, and blue, with jeans being the most important part of the outfit. It was just a fluke that Leah was wearing Levi's and a white shirt today, so technically she qualified, although most of the other contestants (like Nicole) were wearing much more elaborate getups built around U.S. Girls jeans. It wasn't even that they were starting to all look alike — they were starting to look like <u>clones</u>.

I was really bored, my rear end ached, and I was getting hungry, too, when they finally called Nicole. "Go, Nicole!" Courtney and I screamed gratefully.

Up onstage, Nicole's cropped red shirt and the red bandanna in her hair seemed a little less hillbilly than they had in the car. She not only fit right in with everyone else, she even looked pretty cute. Unfortunately, she also looked scared to death. She walked to the end of the runway like a robot, with this terrified expression on her face. (Can robots be terrified? This one was.) At the end she tried to smile, but if anything that look was even scarier. I knew she wouldn't win almost before she turned and walked away. Just glancing at Courtney, I could tell she knew too.

I really felt kind of sorry for Nicole. It took a lot of courage to enter that contest and I don't think she was <u>completely</u> off base. She's tall enough, thin enough, and she has those shocking turquoise eyes. She just doesn't have any presence, or poise, or whatever it is that makes people sit up and take notice. She came and left without a ripple. A couple of girls later, it was as if Nicole had never happened.

And then the announcer called Leah. Leah

practically leapt through the backstage curtains, throwing them wide apart where the other girls had slipped sideways through the opening. She headed straight for the runway, still wearing her faded old Levi's, that loose white button-down, and almost no makeup. She hadn't changed a single thing to improve her chances of winning. Her brown hair swung loose across her shoulders, completely free of red, white, and blue accessories, and I think she was the only contestant there wearing Keds. She walked down the runway like she owned it, not even looking at anyone, and I could feel myself sitting up in my chair. So was everybody else. Whatever that quality is that Nicole doesn't have, Leah has it in buckets.

"Oh my God. She's _good_!" I said, completely blown away.

"She knows how to work an attitude, that's for sure," Courtney told me. "I've never seen anyone look less like they cared in my life."

"I don't think she _does_ care," I said, remembering how little Leah had wanted to enter in the first place.

"Whatever," Courtney said. "It's working."

People were actually clapping, and a bunch of guys were hooting for her. Leah acted like none of it mattered. She reached the end of the runway, barely glanced at the judges, then turned and strode off like a woman with somewhere to go. She pushed back through the curtain without even slowing down. There was barely a pause before the announcer called the next girl, but Courtney and I agreed there was no way we'd want to follow an act like that. I felt even worse for Nicole, thinking how embarrassing it would be to be eclipsed by someone who'd had to be forced into entering the contest. But I still didn't expect things to turn out the way they did. I don't think any of us did.

The last girl finally walked, and the judges fooled around totaling the scores for what felt like an eternity. At last the emcee came out to announce the winner. It was such a shock that it's like I can still hear his whole speech in my mind:

"Ladies and gentlemen! On behalf of the U.S. Girls Clothing Company, it gives me great pleasure to announce our winner, who in addition to taking the title here today has earned an all-expenses-paid trip for four to compete in our national finals in Hollywood, California. Won't you put your hands together for one of the hottest, one of the freshest new faces we've seen this season? Ladies and gentlemen, give it up for Missouri's newest U.S. Girl—<u>Ms. Leah Rosenthal!</u>"

Courtney and I were literally stunned speechless for a couple of seconds, but then we screamed ourselves hoarse. And later, when we saw Nicole, she seemed to be taking the news pretty well. I assume she knew she had no chance anyway, and it's better to have a friend win than a stranger, right? Surprisingly, Leah seemed the least thrilled of us all. She kept saying the whole thing was a big mistake—but maybe she just felt bad about beating Nicole.

In the car on the way home, Courtney tried to tell Leah that she should take the three of us on her free trip to California. Leah said something like she doesn't even know if she'll be going, but of course she will. She probably just doesn't want to take us, which is completely understandable. It's her trip—her guests ought to be her decision.

I still can't believe it happened, though. Leah Rosenthal, U.S. Girl. She made us promise not to tell anyone outside of Eight Prime, but she's dreaming if she thinks she can keep this quiet. This is going to be <u>all</u> over school on Monday.

* * *

I had that dream again, the one where Mom and I are buried in the same grave. I woke up with my heart pounding like crazy and all the sheets soaking wet. My hands were even still clenching like I was going to dig my way out or something. I haven't dreamed that for a while, and I really hoped I was over it. Besides, it seems like if I was going to have some sort of nightmare about Mom, it should have started right after she died. But this one just started a year ago, and it only gets more vivid every time I have it.

I'm standing beside Mom's open grave, looking down into her open casket. I don't think they actually do it like that — I think they always close the casket before they put it in the ground. Maybe if Dad and I had gone to the funeral, my mind would at least get that part right, but I've never even been to the cemetery her parents put her in up in Iowa.

Anyway, I'm standing there, looking down, when all of a sudden the casket closes by itself. The next second I jump into the hole — I have no idea why — and start trying to open the lid again. I can't do it, though, and then all the dirt starts falling in and filling up the grave. I scream, but there's no one to hear me. The dirt's just coming in on its own. And pretty soon I'm trapped with only my head sticking out, and I'm screaming and screaming that I'm not dead, I'm alive. The dirt gets in my mouth, and then it covers my nose and eyes. Everything goes dark, I can't breathe, and it's always at the very last second, when my final bit of air is burning in my lungs, that I wake up and gasp like I really <u>haven't</u> breathed the whole time. I don't know — maybe I haven't. I wonder if it's possible to hold your breath in a dream like that. Maybe someday I won't breathe until I really do pass out. That's a pretty scary thought. The dream is scary enough without having to worry about that, too.

All things considered, I think I like my other nightmare better — the one where I'm naked in study hall. It's totally embarrassing, but at least no one else ever seems to notice. I can't believe I have to choose between being buried alive or studying naked, though. I'm pretty sure that can't be normal.

* * *

MONDAY
You will not believe what happened today! Jesse got suspended for having liquor in his gym locker. Coach Davis caught him with it after

Friday's game. I couldn't get more details, because no one's talked to Jesse, but that much of the story is all over school. I don't know who leaked it—probably one of the football players. From there it went to the cheerleaders, and from there to the rest of the world. I don't even know if everyone else in Eight Prime knows yet, but if they don't, they will.

I just can't believe he could be so stupid! I mean, I figured he had a problem, but how dumb do you have to be to bring alcohol to school? I guess he'll have to shape up now, though. He's been suspended for a week, and the rumor is he might even get cut from the team.

What a pitiful way to steal the spotlight from Leah. I thought today was going to be all about her winning the modeling contest, and I never heard a word about that. Instead it was all Jesse. Jesse, Jesse, Jesse.

I'll tell you the truth—I don't even feel sorry for him. He totally brought this on himself.

* * *

TUESDAY
I was walking out to the main road this morning when Jesse drove up in his BMW and asked me if I wanted a ride. I couldn't believe my

eyes. He didn't even have the good sense to look embarrassed.

"I thought you were suspended," I said.

"I'm pretty sure I'm still allowed to use the city streets," he said sarcastically. "Unless, of course, you'd _rather_ ride the bus."

I don't even know why I got in his car. All I can say is, I must really hate riding the bus. "What I meant was, why are you going to school?" I asked as he made a U-turn in our road.

"I'm _not_ going to school," he said. "I was just out driving around, so I thought I'd cruise by. That's all."

He must think I'm stupid if he honestly expected me to believe such a lame story. I didn't even comment.

"Does, uh, does everyone in Eight Prime know what happened?" he asked, a little nervously.

"What do you think?" I said. "The entire school knows."

"So then I guess everyone thinks I'm an idiot for getting caught with liquor in my locker?"

I just shrugged. Isn't it obvious? Even people who drink think he's an idiot for getting _caught_. He's not going to get any sympathy from me.

"Listen, Melanie, do you think you could cut me a little slack?" he said, all crabby, like _I_ was the cause of his troubles. "Do you think I don't know what a moron I am? I've barely slept at all since I got busted Friday night, so believe me, I've had plenty of time to figure it out."

"Well, you are a moron," I told him. "Do you have a drinking problem or what?"

"No, I don't have a problem."

"Then why have liquor at school, Jesse? And what about getting drunk at that party and making an idiot of Nicole? Or how about after the Cave Creek game, when I had to—" I almost said "slap you," but I'm pretty sure he could fill in the blank.

"Like you're such an expert on drinking problems," he scoffed.

If he only knew. But my family secrets are none of his business. "If you don't want my opinion, then why did you ask?" I said instead.

"I didn't ask you _that_."

"Fine," I said. But it wasn't, and we both knew it. I couldn't wait to get out of his car. I really didn't think he'd say anything else to me. I sure didn't plan to talk to him. But right before we got to school he surprised me with one last question.

"Do the Junior Explorers know?" he asked. "Has anyone told Jason?"

I have to admit I didn't see that coming, and I

actually thought it was kind of sweet that he was worried about Jason's feelings. That little boy took to him right away when he found out Jesse was a real CCHS Wildcat, so hearing about this might be kind of a blow, especially to a kid who doesn't need any more disappointment. If I messed up like that, I sure wouldn't want Amy to find out. It's not exactly role-model material.

"No, I don't think so," I said. "I don't see why anyone would tell the Junior Explorers."

"I don't want Jason to know, and I'm quitting Eight Prime," he said. "Could you tell Peter for me?"

I was absolutely stunned. That's his big solution? That's how he plans to fix everything? That's so _Jesse_!

"No, I won't tell Peter for you," I snapped. "Tell him yourself, you big quitter!"

"Oh, that's mature," he said.

"And I suppose bailing out on someone you've promised to help is all grown up!" I shot back. "You make me _sick_!"

He tried to say something else, but he'd just pulled to the curb in front of school and I jumped out before he could. "I'm not talking to you!" I yelled, slamming his door. I mean it, too. I am _not_ talking to him.

What a weasel. To think that I felt <u>sorry</u> for him at the game last Friday! I should have saved my energy. Jesse Jones will never change. He'll always be the same vain, selfish, spoiled piece of work he ever was. I am <u>so</u> glad I never let him near me. And I never, ever will!

This journal belongs to:

Leah Rosenthal

4519 South Sycamore, #410

Clearwater Crossing, Missouri

(573) 555-2983

There are times when I honestly think it would be better not to keep a journal. Today, for instance, I really have to wonder if I'm going to want to remember any of this stuff when I'm old. For that matter, I doubt I'll want to remember it next week. I wish I had never gone to St. Louis or even heard of U.S. Girls! When Daryl finds out I won a modeling contest, she'll probably die laughing. She'll probably die laughing when she finds out I <u>entered</u>. I like my new friends in Eight Prime, but none of them seems to understand how not-like-me modeling is. The worst part is, Miguel gets it least of all. We are so close now that I can't imagine not being with him, but there are still times I'd give anything if Daryl hadn't moved to Chicago. The last time I saw her last summer already feels so long ago it's like we were best friends in a different life. I've nearly forgotten what she looks like.

At least no one at school is giving me a hard time about the contest, because all the attention's been on Jesse. I'd thank him, if that wouldn't seem so cynical. I'm obviously sorry he got in trouble; it's just that if it was going to happen anyway, his timing is excellent. I was dreading school yesterday, thinking everyone would be coming up and congratulating me on winning the contest (and expecting me to be happy about it). I hate situations like that, where people think they're being nice and you just want to curl up and die. I swore Eight Prime to secrecy; no one is supposed to know except us and Courtney. But with so many other people at the mall, it seems awfully likely that at least <u>one</u> of them was from our school, and I was positive the news was going to spread like a fatal disease.

[I feel like I ought to state for the record that I don't think a modeling contest or the fact that I won it is in any way a big deal or even <u>worth</u> talking about. But in a town this small, things tend to get blown out of proportion. The entire school knew Jesse had been suspended within an hour of it happening. In Los Angeles you could probably rob a liquor store and keep it quiet; here you can't even cut your hair. I love Clearwater Crossing. I'm glad I grew up here. But I'm definitely not going to Clearwater University. Aside from the obvious drawback of having both my parents teaching there, a person needs to branch out sometime.]

Anyway, poor Jesse took all the heat yesterday, and he was still a hot topic today. His suspension is turning into a big debate. Even Eight Prime was talking about him at lunchtime, and we're his friends. The whole group except Melanie (and Jesse, obviously) ended up at one table, but even we couldn't agree on how badly he'd messed up and whether or not his punishment is fair. I was hoping someone might have heard from him, so that we'd have the story straight from the source, but he hasn't called any of us. Everyone's talking about him, but I still haven't found anyone who's actually talked <u>to</u> him.

"We don't know anything new, then?" I asked.

"Well, he's still suspended," Ben told me, trying to be helpful.

"No kidding," Miguel muttered.

[For the record, Miguel was in one of his moods today. He was joking around off and on, like he was trying to hide it, but I could tell something was bugging him. I <u>hate</u> it when he gets all moody on me! It's not like I think he shouldn't have emotions, but I hate how he never shares them. It's so stoic and macho and pointless.]

"I wonder if one of us ought to call him," Jenna said.

"I've been going back and forth with that too," Peter said. "I'd like to make sure he's okay, but I don't want to embarrass him. Maybe he's not ready to talk about it yet."

"It's got to be hard for him," Miguel pointed out. "The guy practically lives for football."

"I think we should call him," Jenna said. "It's got

to be better to call and maybe embarrass him a little than let him think we don't care."

"I'll do it," Nicole offered right away. She had Courtney with her, as usual, but C. was the only non-Eight-Primer at the table. "We definitely ought to call and let Jesse know we support him, that we're behind him one hundred percent."

"Well, I don't know how much we _support_ him," Jenna said, frowning slightly. "I mean, we sure don't condone what he did. I just thought we ought to tell him we're still his friends."

"Right," Peter said. "Everyone makes a mistake sometime."

"Getting caught with liquor in your locker is a bigger mistake than most," Miguel said. I think he feels kind of bad for Jesse, but he doesn't agree with what he did, either. Most people are looking at this as one dumb act by a single person, but being on the water polo team, Miguel sees it more from that perspective, like Jesse brought the whole team down.

Nicole's one of the few people who doesn't seem to think Jesse did anything wrong at all. "Don't you see? That's the only difference!" she said. "Everyone drinks. Jesse was just unlucky enough to get caught!"

"Or stupid enough," Courtney muttered. I got the feeling she doesn't like him very much, but I don't know why she wouldn't.

"I don't drink," Peter said.

"Me either," said Jenna. "I mean, I wouldn't have anything against it if we were old enough, but it's against the law for minors to have alcohol. Not only that, but Jesse broke school rules—"

"Oh, _please!_" Nicole broke in. "You can't be serious. Everyone breaks the rules."

"I don't," Peter said.

"Me either," Jenna echoed.

"I could have told you _that_," Courtney said under her breath. On second thought, maybe Courtney was just in a bad mood today too. There was a lot of that going around.

Nicole started to take her case to Ben, then seemed to realize how pointless that was (because he's not exactly Mr. Cool). She turned to me instead, but I refuse to be pulled in. Nicole may have a point, but so do Peter and Jenna. The truth is I'm not sure _how_ I feel. The important thing is that how I feel about what Jesse did doesn't change how I feel about Jesse, especially since I don't believe he hurt anyone but himself. It would be different if there were other people involved, like he was driving drunk or something.

"You've all got to be kidding me," Nicole said indignantly.

"Look, Nicole," said Peter, "we have different opinions about what Jesse did, but that's not really important. What's done is done, and I'm sure he regrets it. We only want him to know that we aren't sitting around judging him for it."

"It sounds like you're judging him to me!" Nicole said.

"Maybe _I_ should make the phone call," I offered. "I think I know what to say."

"No! I'll do it," Nicole insisted. "I'll just tell him that we miss him, and that we're all still his friends. All right? Can everyone agree on that at least?"

The bell rang then, and Nicole said she was going to call Jesse after school. The rest of us grabbed our things and scattered for fifth period—my least favorite class. The _only_ good thing about biology with Ms. Walker is that that's where I met Miguel. In fact, Miguel informed me today that he doesn't think he and I would have ever met if Ms. Walker hadn't irritated me into making a pretty big scene the first week of school.

"You don't think so?" I asked. "Not even after all this time?"

"Probably not," he said. "And besides, what would my chances be now? I mean, now that you're a U.S. Girl?"

I couldn't believe it. None of my other friends even brings it up, and my boyfriend rubs my nose in it. I've told him and told him how embarrassing this whole thing is to me, but he refuses to listen.

"I'm going out with a model," he sang, flipping my French braid around.

"I'm warning you, Miguel," I said.

"Aw, come on, Leah. You ought to be proud," he told me. "_I'm_ proud, and I didn't even win."

I tried not to, but I had to smile; he made it sound like he'd been a contestant. "And all of Missouri can be thankful for that. I don't think you'd have done too well in the swimsuit competition."

"There was a swimsuit competition?" he said, all excited. "You didn't tell me that!"

"I was kidding! Can we please change the subject?"

"You're not still thinking of dropping out of the finals, are you?" he asked, ignoring my request. "That would be a big mistake. Forget that you'd break Nicole's heart. What about the scholarship?"

He had to mention the scholarship. Never in a million years would I have expected to hear myself complaining about a scholarship, but it's the only thing that's keeping me from dropping out of the U.S. Girls finals, which is what I'd desperately like to do. I wouldn't mind taking a free trip to California, but when I finally see the West Coast I want to check out the sights and schools, not compete in some lame beauty pageant. I let Nicole talk me into doing that contest without even knowing there were prizes other than the modeling contract (which I never expected to win). I knew I didn't want the contract, so driving home from St. Louis I made up my mind to call the contest organizers Monday and let the runner-up take my place. Then on Sunday, just for the heck of it, I read that load of literature they shoved into my arms before I left the mall. The final five winners are getting scholarships of $15,000 a year. _Each_. For four years. My parents do all right as professors, and I know they've been saving for my education, but with schools like Stanford and Harvard on my wish list, I can't afford to ignore that kind of money.

I will never forget what Nicole said when I called to ask if she knew the ultimate winners got enormous scholarships.

"Um, yeah," she answered. "I think so. But hey, did you see the part about the _facials_? Free facials every week for a _year_, and free haircuts and makeup too! Is that the best or what?"

I like Nicole, but I don't think we have a lot in common.

So of course I had to tell Miguel that I wasn't dropping out of the finals, and he started teasing me about how he was dating a model again until I got really irritated. "I don't even want to go out with you if that's the only reason you're dating me," I said.

"Luckily for me you know it isn't," he said, not missing a beat. "Because I was dating you before you won."

And that's the most irritating thing of all. I've always kept a pretty low profile at school. Not too many people know who I am, and that's the way I like it. Miguel, on the other hand, is like some sort of CCHS heartthrob. <u>Everyone</u> knows who he is, especially the girls. The thing that kills me is that we still haven't told people we're a couple, and now, when we finally do, the entire school is going to think he only likes me because of that stupid contest and how I look. That's <u>not</u> why he likes me. He likes me because I'm smart, and real, and I tell him the truth (even when it hurts). He likes me for my personality.

Who's going to believe that now? The way he was acting today, <u>I</u> barely even believe it. I wish I had never, ever, <u>ever</u> heard of U.S. Girls!

I am dead! I was minding my own business, trying to read the newspaper before Mom and Dad got home, when Nicole called in a complete panic and told me to switch to Channel 7. The television wasn't on, and I didn't want to watch it anyway. "What's up?" I asked her.

"What's up?" she repeated, so excited she almost yelled. "You're on the news, that's all!"

I hung up in a hurry and dove for the remote, only to find that someone had taped my victory walk at the

U.S. Girls competition, complete with two dozen roses and that goofy tiara they made me wear. I just about shriveled up and died. So much for keeping things quiet; tomorrow the whole school will know for sure.

If that's not bad enough, the news anchor made a completely smarmy speech over the pictures, something like: "Local beauty Leah Rosenthal took St. Louis by storm in the U.S. Girls national model search held there this past weekend. The winsome seventeen-year-old student from Clearwater Crossing High School is said to have held the audience breathless."

Is that nauseating, or what? Why doesn't he just pass out ammunition?

"_Who_ said that?" I think I yelled. I mean, honestly. Winsome? Who even _says_ winsome? I am never going to live this down. Everyone is going to tease and embarrass me and make a big deal for the rest of my life.

But that's not all. No, believe it or not, it gets _worse_. I had barely turned the TV off when Nicole called again. "Wasn't that outrageous?" she gushed. "I got most of it on tape, if you want a copy. I can't _wait_ for school tomorrow—everyone's going to be so excited! I know you said you didn't want us to spread this around, but since the whole town just saw it on the news, I guess we can talk about it now. Right?"

Like I could stop her. It's a miracle she's lasted this long.

"I didn't even know they had TV cameras there, did you?" she asked, talking a mile a minute. "I mean, I guess it could have been home video, but the picture was really good. I wish they'd shown your first walk, though, because that was the one I missed. If they hadn't made us all—"

"Nicole," I tried to interrupt because I was getting another call, but her mouth had so much momentum I'm not sure superglue could have stopped it.

"—stand behind that stupid stage, then I might have been able to see you. That was really kind of dumb, when you think about it. There wasn't any reason—"

"Nicole—" I tried again.

"—to keep us all back there. They could have let us sit in the audience after we'd had our turn. Then we'd at least have gotten to see some of the other contestants. All I got to see was the back of that stupid stage, and—"

"Nicole!" I finally shouted. "There's someone on Call Waiting. Can't you hear that clicking?"

I said I had to take the call because I thought it might be Mom or Dad. "Okay. I'll hold," she said. I had meant to hang up, but there wasn't time to argue, so I just said okay and pressed the button for the second line.

"May I speak to Leah Rosenthal, please?" this woman asked. I think she was trying to sound cultured, but she came off like she'd been taking diction lessons from Thurston Howell III.

"This is Leah," I said cautiously.

"Oh, splendid. Leah, my name is Kristell Lawrence, and I'm the director of marketing for U.S. Girls, St. Louis. The reason I'm calling is to give you some _wonderful_ news. The Missouri U.S. Girls stores are _so_ excited about our new campaign, and they really like your look. We want you to do a photo shoot this Thursday for some local advertising. Isn't that great?"

"I go to school on Thursdays," I told her, but Kristell only laughed.

"Of course you do, dear," she said (very condescendingly, I could add). "We're not completely inexperienced with this sort of thing, you know. Now listen, I have it all set up. Do you have a little something to write on?"

I got a pen and pad off the counter, and Kristell gave me the address of a photo studio downtown. "Now, don't forget, they're expecting you at four," she said. "That should give you plenty of time to get there _after_ school. Be sure to bring lots of shirts, too. They'll have the jeans, of course, but I don't know what they'll want you to wear on top. Maybe nothing!"

"I am _not_—" I started. Can you imagine? But Kristell was just yanking my chain.

"It was a joke, dear. Kidding! Anyway, I've got to fly. Congratulations, and have a great time Thursday." She hung up before I could say another word.

"Of all the nerve!" I exclaimed. "She never even asked if I'd do it!"

"Do what?" Nicole asked eagerly. I had completely forgotten she was holding on the other line. I really didn't feel like explaining, and I had to take a few deep breaths before I could even answer.

"That was some woman named Kristell," I told her. "U.S. Girls is having a stupid photo shoot on Thursday and she basically just ordered me to be there. She didn't even ask if I wanted to go."

"Oh, Leah!" she cried. "Oh, wow! How exciting!"

I don't want to offend her, but Nicole and I don't see eye to eye on this modeling thing at all. I suppose there's nothing _wrong_ with modeling, if that's what you want to do. It's just not what _I_ want to do. It's embarrassing to have people stare at you like you're some sort of thing instead of a person. It's demeaning. And besides, if I ever get famous, I want it to be for doing something wonderful, not for wearing clothes.

"Can I go with you?" Nicole begged. "I'll stay out of

the way, and I promise I won't be a pest. Oh, please, Leah. _Please?_ I've never seen a photo shoot before."

I actually don't know if I'm supposed to bring anyone or not, but I told her she could come. If having Nicole there makes the U.S. Girls people mad, what do I care? It's not like I asked to do their shoot. If I could give my title to Nicole somehow, I'd do it in a second. Plus, after our discussion the other day, I'm pretty sure she'd be thrilled to do all the modeling and leave the scholarship to me. Everyone would win.

"This is going to be so cool!" she said. "Do you want to borrow anything of mine? I have tons of hair clips and headbands and things like that. Hey! I could help you do your hair if you want! And your makeup! I didn't want to say anything before, but you wore hardly any at the contest. For photos they're going to want more. Have you seen that new look on the runway models, with the jewel-toned eye shadows up to the brow?"

That's all I need: Nicole loose on my face with some bright blue powder. I know she means well, but does it ever even occur to her that different people have different styles? I don't _want_ to look like a runway model. For that matter, I'm pretty sure those women don't go to the grocery store looking like that.

I can't believe I got into this situation. I feel like

I'm betraying myself just by staying in the contest. But if I drop out, won't that be betraying myself even worse? I've been looking forward to college ever since second grade. Like I said before, I know Mom and Dad will send me to the best school they can afford—but the Ivy League is kind of out of ours.

On the other hand, I could go to L.A., compete in the stupid contest, and lose (in fact, the odds are seriously in favor of that). After all this agonizing, I'd still come away with squat.

So what am I going to do? It makes my head ache just thinking about it.

10/21

Today was even more embarrassing than I predicted. People who don't know me at all saw me on the news and were acting like my new best friends. It was ridiculous. Some girl I never met before started talking to me in the hallway, followed me into the girls' room, and practically came into my stall. I had to shut the door in her face.

I tried to tell Miguel about it at lunchtime, but he was no help whatsoever. "Ah, the trials of the rich and famous," he said. [Which, for the record, sounded sarcastic to me.]

"I'm hardly rich or famous," I retorted. "But I do feel like I'm on trial. It seems like everyone's checking me out every second. What I'm doing, what I'm wearing, just everything."

"I love what you're wearing," he told me. "Probably five or six different girls are going to show up at school in that exact same outfit tomorrow."

I groaned at the mere thought. "I'm just not ready for this," I said. "I don't mean to sound conceited, or ungrateful, but I never thought I'd be doing something so— "

"Hey! Hi, guys!" Ben shouted right behind us. I wish he wouldn't sneak up like that. He does it all the time, but today I was already so on edge he nearly gave me a heart attack. Plus Miguel was sitting real close, for once, and the second he saw Ben he scooted to twice his usual distance. No public displays for Miguel. Especially since no one is supposed to know about us. [For the record, that idea was really more his than mine.]

"I've been looking for you everywhere!" Ben said, dropping onto the grass beside us. "I saw you on TV, Leah. And everyone's talking about you in all my classes. How come when you told me about the contest, you made it sound like it wasn't a big deal?"

"Because I didn't want it to be," I answered.

"But it _is_," Ben said, turning from me to Miguel. "Isn't it?"

"Apparently so," Miguel said dryly. I think he's finally starting to understand what I've been worried about all along. Every time he tried to talk to me today it seemed like at least five people broke in on us. At lunch, for example, we'd already been interrupted by Ben, and the next thing I knew Nicole came running too.

"There you are, Leah!" she cried, like I've been missing for a week. "I've been searching all over for you! Look what I brought you," she said, handing me a ripped-out magazine page and pointing to the model. "That's what I was talking about yesterday. See how they do that with the eye shadow?"

Like I could miss it. The poor girl looked like someone had socked her in both eyes. Before I could think of a nice way to tell Nicole I won't be making a similar fashion statement tomorrow, though, three of Miguel's water polo friends came over and joined us. [See? Five interruptions.] I'd never met any of them before today, but their timing was strictly coincidence, right?

"Hi there!" the one named Derrick said directly to me, this really smug look on his face. "I didn't know you knew this guy," he added, nodding toward Miguel.

"I didn't know I knew you," I said. His buddies laughed, but Derrick was either dumb or deluded enough to still believe I might be interested.

"That's exactly the oversight I'm here to correct," he said with this fake velvet voice, like some cheap lounge act. The guy obviously thinks he's Mr. Smooth, which is almost more sad than funny. Maybe I should have flirted back, just to let Miguel see what happens when everyone thinks a girl is single, but it's just not me to do something like that. I can think of it (usually way after the fact), but actually doing it would be so dishonest.

Anyway, these guys all congratulated me on winning the contest, and then they started asking me modeling questions (like I know the answers). They were completely obvious about the fact that they had come to talk to me, not Miguel; him being there was just a convenient excuse. I don't think he much liked sitting by while they hit on me, but he could have stopped it with a few simple words. He didn't. If I say that I was actually relieved to go to biology, that ought to sum up how uncomfortable the whole situation was.

Walking to class, Miguel said he had something to ask me, and did I want to go to the lake after school? The lake's kind of our special spot, since it's where we first kissed, and normally I'd have jumped at the invitation. Right now, though, there are just too many things going on, so I tried to get him to ask me whatever it was in the hallway.

He glanced around at the crowd and shook his head. "I'd rather ask you there," he said.

"Well, I can't go," I told him. "I've got a stupid

photo shoot for U.S. Girls tomorrow after school. That means that this afternoon I have to get ahead on my homework and figure out what clothes to take."

"Leah, that's great!" he said, all excited. "What are the pictures for? Why didn't you tell me before?"

"I don't know what the pictures are for. Some ad," I said. [Is it too much to hope it will only run in foreign countries?] "And I didn't mention it before because I don't even want to do it. This whole modeling thing is stressing me out."

"You're going to do great," he said, like that's the part I'm worried about. "I'm so proud of you."

It's like I was saying before—he thinks he's being nice. He probably got that reassuring smile right out of Supportive Boyfriend 101. I'd like it a whole lot better if he got jealous, threw a big fit, and said he doesn't want me modeling anymore.

I would _love_ that, in fact. It's not like I'd ever actually let him tell me what to do, but right now I'm just looking for any excuse. Besides, he's so cute when he thinks he's in charge.

I just got back from that photo shoot, and I could fill up the rest of this book on the subject of how embarrassing that was. In the car on the way home, though, I decided to block it out. If I pretend it didn't happen long enough, I can only hope that eventually I'll forget it completely. I'm certainly not going to put myself through it twice by writing it all down here. In the interest of keeping a complete record, though, I'll jot down the key points:

1. Nicole was a modeling menace, telling me what to do, how to pose, and practically how to breathe.
2. They made me wear a shirt that looked like two handkerchiefs knotted over my navel. (I gave it to Nicole afterwards. She was thrilled.)
3. They painted me up to look <u>worse</u> than Nicole's magazine.
4. The photographer was like a character out of <u>La Cage Aux Folles</u>.
5. Even my own mother told me to think of the scholarship.

I'm pretty sure that's all I want to say about that, and that's all I have time for anyway. There's an Eight Prime meeting at Nicole's tonight and I barely have time to eat and shower before I have to leave.

I just got home from Nicole's. Would you believe she wore that shirt I gave her from the photo shoot? I'm glad she likes it, but she couldn't even have washed it yet. Not to mention that it shows half your belly and this is October. She had the heat in that basement cranked up so high that I'll probably have to shower again before I go to bed. On the plus side, though, she put out a great buffet, with more food than eight people could possibly eat after dinner. Or seven, I should say, since Jesse didn't make it. From what she said, Nicole was obviously under the impression he'd be there, but Melanie finally told us she didn't think he was coming.

"Why?" Peter asked.

"Has he talked to you at all?" Melanie answered. [Which, for the record, isn't an answer.]

"No," Peter said. "I haven't seen him all week. Have you?"

"I just think we should start, that's all. If he shows up, he shows up." Melanie crossed and uncrossed her legs a few times, which totally gave her away. She was hiding something, but I don't know what. I mean, it's no secret Jesse's suspended, so his parents probably just wouldn't let him come. I don't know what's so secret about that.

Ben rushed over to the couch with his plate in his hands and BBQ sauce all over his face. "Are we starting?" he asked. "Because I have big news!" Nicole said she guessed we might as well, so everyone sat down.

"I got us a building for the haunted house!" Ben announced, so proud of himself he was practically bursting. "My dad's company, ComAm, has an old storehouse down by the railroad tracks, and there's nothing in it right now. They said we can use it for our fund-raiser if we clean up afterward and don't make any permanent changes."

"Ben! That's great!" Jenna cried.

Everyone else was excited too.

"And they know we're going to build sets and everything?" Peter asked. "I mean, we can't promise that no one will spill paint or something by accident."

Ben smiled. "That's the beauty—they don't care! It's just a warehouse with brick walls and a bare concrete floor. They use it to store their excess inventory before they ship it on the train, and right now it's completely empty."

It's really more perfect than we could have hoped for. Not only did we get a building, but by the tracks is a great location. Everyone started talking at once, shouting out their ideas. Peter wanted to figure out a schedule for extra meetings so that everything gets done in time. Melanie thought we ought to get a notice in the newspaper right away. Jenna started trying to divide everyone into committees.

"I think we ought to stay open three nights," Peter said. "Halloween's on a Saturday this year, so we could hold the haunted house on Thursday, Friday, and Saturday."

"Why not longer?" Ben asked. "I can get the key to the building tomorrow."

Peter thought we'd be lucky to get done in time to open Thursday, though (which is exactly a week away), so we decided to go with his three-night schedule. We'll be working on setting things up this weekend. Jenna and I are doing flyers, signs, banners, and tickets. Ben's in charge of the building—getting the key and arranging things with ComAm. Peter's coordinating publicity and volunteers. Miguel's in charge of building the sets, and since Jesse wasn't there he got assigned to help Miguel. Melanie is our chief painter/decorator, and Nicole's in charge of costumes. [Whew! When I write it all out, it seems like even more work.]

Anyway, it was a good meeting and we got a lot done, even without Jesse. I hope he's coming Saturday, though, because we're going to need all the help we can get. Maybe someone should call him and make sure. I could mention it to Nicole, since she's the one who called him before. On the other hand, she didn't know what was going on with him tonight, and I'm pretty sure Melanie did, so maybe Melanie should make the call. Well, I'm not going to worry about it. <u>Somebody</u> will tell him.

I just looked at the clock and it's nearly midnight, so I think I'll skip that second shower and go to bed now. If tomorrow's another day like this one, I'm going to need my strength.

The Wildcats are playing the Mapleton Mavericks tonight, but it's an away game and Miguel and I decided not to go. I never went to games at all last year, so that's no big sacrifice in my book, especially since Miguel and I will be together all day tomorrow. I don't know why he didn't want to go, but Mapleton is pretty far and I don't think there's any real question about us winning. Maybe it didn't seem worth the trip. He said he was just going to stay home and hang out with his mom and his sister, Rosa — whom I _also_ haven't met.

This keeping ourselves a secret thing has gotten out of hand. At first, right after we got together, everything was so new that it was also kind of scary. We agreed that it might be better to keep things quiet awhile. I thought it might make the other people in Eight Prime feel odd if Miguel and I suddenly became a couple, and there wasn't anyone else I wanted to tell. Except for Mom and Dad, of course, and they've known a long time. They still haven't met him yet, though. They were supposed to once, that time we were all going to brunch, but Miguel weaseled out of that and I never managed to set it up again. [For the record, I'm positive Miguel's afraid to meet them, in case they don't like him or something. I already told him they will, but I obviously didn't convince him. He can be so weird about the simplest things sometimes.]

At least they <u>know</u> about him, though. Miguel's mom still doesn't know I exist, and I can't figure out why he won't tell her.

I hope he's not still worrying about that religion thing, because it couldn't matter less to anyone but him. He honestly thought my dad wouldn't like him being Catholic, since Dad's Jewish. Mom's Lutheran, though, and Dad <u>married</u> her, so he's obviously not that prejudiced. Besides, what difference does it make, since none of them ever go to church or temple anyway? If Miguel was in a seminary or something, then it might be more important—although probably only to him. Come to think of it, if he were studying to be a priest, the whole girlfriend thing would be kind of moot.

Maybe I'm making too big a deal about this, but it bugs me. I mean, if I really am his girlfriend, shouldn't I meet his family? I'm starting to feel like he must be ashamed of me.

Or maybe he's the one that's ashamed—of where he lives. If he is, he shouldn't be, though. It's not his fault his family's in public housing, since his dad died three years ago without any health insurance. I don't know many details, except that Mr. del Rios had cancer and by the time he was diagnosed he was terminal. Losing the man of the family and being hit with all those medical bills must have been hard on them financially as well as emotionally.

The problem is, Miguel thinks I don't know where he lives. He's gone to a lot of trouble to hide it, actually, and if I hadn't gotten so fed up with his evasions that I followed him home on the sly, I still wouldn't have a clue. I'd love to tell him I know, and that it doesn't matter at all. If I did, I'd have to tell him _how_ I know, though, and that could get pretty tricky. It'll be a lot better if he just tells me himself. I assume he plans to tell me _sometime_.

The trouble with Miguel is, sometimes it feels like assuming is all I do.

10/24

I'm exhausted, but I feel good, too. We got a ton of work done on the haunted house today. When we first showed up, everyone kind of stood there looking around that empty warehouse, and I think we were all wondering how we'd ever pull it off. But then the volunteers started flooding in, and stuff started happening. We had people from Jenna's church, and from the CCHS drama department. Chris Hobart brought a bunch of college friends. Pretty soon there were hammers banging and sawdust flying everywhere and Miguel was running around like crazy trying to keep everyone on track with the construction plan he'd drawn up. Caitlin was there to help Jenna and me set up the ticket-taking area, but Nicole got stuck in charge of a bunch of borrowed costume stuff, so I decided to help her.

"I don't know why they expect me to figure out what everyone else has to dress up as," she complained, digging through the heap of clothes. I was actually surprised she wasn't more into it; I would have thought costume director was right up her alley.

"Someone has to be in charge," I reminded her. "Otherwise we could end up with costumes that don't fit our theme, or people dressed the same way. What have you got so far?"

Nicole rolled her eyes. "A pile of junk, is what it looks like. I don't even know what all's in here."

We decided to make an inventory before we passed anything out, since Eight Prime is responsible for getting everything back to the drama department. There was a cloak Nicole thought would make a good Dracula cape, and a whole bunch of shawls with no obvious use. Then Nicole held up a beautiful gown of gold satin and ivory lace. "I have _no_ idea what to do with this," she said. "It's pretty, but we're putting on a haunted house, not <u>Hamlet</u>."

"I'll wear it," I offered instantly.

"It's not exactly scary," she said.

I have a great idea for it, though. I can hardly wait to try it.

"I'll make it scary, trust me," I said, taking an ivory lace shawl to go with it. "Besides, that's one costume you can cross off your list, <u>and</u> one less shawl to deal with."

"Suit yourself," she said with a shrug.

We went through the rest of the pile and Nicole ended up picking a black dress for herself before walking around handing out the other stuff she'd found uses for. I noticed that Jesse got the cape, but most of the other things looked like fairly basic black clothes. She's still got a lot of accessorizing to do before those clothes turn into costumes.

Oh, and we're going to be in the newspaper! Peter's dad got a reporter to come out from <u>The Clearwater Herald</u>. She interviewed Peter, and then she took our picture behind the building. I don't know how much will actually get into the paper, but if they're short on space I hope they give us an article and forget the photo. As far as I'm concerned, they can forget the photo anyway.

In the afternoon, I mostly helped Miguel and the

construction crew. I convinced Ben to stop trying to hammer nails (which made me a hero with the other, more coordinated guys) and he and I stacked leftover wood into piles by size, so it could be used for other things. Then we went around sweeping up sawdust and making sure there weren't nails on the floor.

The last thing I did, right as it was getting dark, was carry a bunch of armloads of wood scraps to the Dumpster out back with Miguel. "I don't know about you, but I'm exhausted," I told him.

"It's all this getting your picture taken," he teased. "How many modeling jobs does that make so far this month?"

He just can't give it a rest.

I asked if he wanted to get together tomorrow, and since that's a Sunday I figured he'd be free. I know from that time I snuck around following him that he helps his mom with errands on Saturday mornings [for the record, I _really_ wish I hadn't done that], but his Sundays should be wide open, since he doesn't go to mass anymore.

"All right," he said. "How about I pick you up in the morning and we hike around the lake? All the leaves are turning color up there."

"No, not the lake," I said. "We always go to the lake."

He looked surprised, and I can see now how that might have sounded mean. But _I_ was the one who asked _him_ to do something, and I had something different in mind.

"Why don't I come to your house?" I said. "We could just hang out and relax." I thought I made it sound casual, but he got in a sweat right away.

"No. That's not such a good idea," he said, all flustered. "It's, um, going to be Sunday, and my mom and Rosa will be at mass half the day. At least."

"I don't mind," I said.

"Well, she will," he insisted. "I told you my mom's old-fashioned. She'd have a fit if she knew I had a girl alone in the house with me."

"But we're alone together all the time!"

"Not in my bedroom," he said.

"Who said we had to be in your bedroom? We could stay in the living room, or the kitchen."

"Leah, what's the point?" he said. "There's nothing to do at my house."

I knew what the real problem was, though. He wasn't worried about his mom seeing me in his bedroom—he was worried about her seeing me at all. It made me mad, I have to admit.

"Look, can we talk about this later?" he said, glancing around the empty parking lot like somebody might hear me. "I don't want the whole world to know our business."

"You don't want them to know we _have_ business!" I said. "Why are you keeping us a secret, Miguel? Are you that ashamed of me?"

"Me?" he protested. "You didn't want to tell anyone either. You thought it would make everyone in Eight Prime feel weird if they knew we were a couple, remember?"

"That was then!" I practically shouted. "Do you think they haven't guessed by now that something's going on? Melanie caught us that day in the library, and the rest of them see us together everywhere. They must know we're hiding something, and I think it's time we tell them."

He looked down at his feet. "I want to tell them too. I just thought maybe we could do it at the Homecoming dance."

"You mean you thought that if we showed up as each other's dates and danced a few slow dances together we wouldn't actually have to _tell_ anyone," I accused, certain I was right. That's just so like Miguel. He hates to talk about _anything_.

Miguel shrugged, his eyes still on the ground. "So you don't want to go to the dance with me, then?"

"Of course I want to go," I said (although I wouldn't have minded if his invitation had been a little more romantic). Before I could say anything else, though, Peter came out of the warehouse, followed by everyone else. They were done for the night and wanted to lock up. I don't think anyone heard us arguing. I hope not, because as much as I want them to know about us now, that's not how I want them to find out.

Everyone started wandering down to the street. "Don't forget," Peter yelled after us. "Ask your parents if at least one of them can chaperone on at least one night."

"My mom couldn't possibly spend four hours here, standing outside in the cold," Miguel said as he let us into his car. "I'm not even going to ask her."

That would have rubbed me wrong even if I wasn't already kind of mad at him. It's okay for everyone else's parents, but not his? He just doesn't want to bring his mom because then I might actually meet her. I was so irritated that I barely talked to him for the rest of the ride, so now I don't know if we're doing anything tomorrow or not. We never actually made a plan, and he hasn't called since he dropped me off (not that he ever does). I bet I won't see him until Monday.

You know what? That's just fine. In a lot of ways meeting Miguel is the best thing that ever happened to me. But sometimes I wonder: Does being so wrapped up with him mean I'm missing out on something else? Because I promised myself I'd never miss anything for a guy. Ever. So I won't sit around pining *if he doesn't call me tomorrow. I'll hang out with Mom and write a letter to Daryl and get started on that new Dead Sea Scrolls book. I could always call Jenna, too, and see what she's doing. Or better yet, I'll make up those haunted-house tickets and flyers and get them printed out.*

It's not like I can't keep myself entertained. I have a <u>hundred</u> things to do.

10/25

Look what I cut out of this morning's paper!

HAUNTED HOUSE AIDS WORTHY CAUSE
Local Teens Remember Classmate
By Susan Graham
Staff Writer

CLEARWATER CROSSING—This Halloween, when many will be thinking only of candy and parties, eight former classmates of deceased Clearwater Crossing High School student Kurt Englbehrt will be working to make a difference. Peter Altmann, Melanie Andrews, Jenna Conrad, Leah Rosenthal, Ben Pipkin, Miguel del Rios, Jesse Jones, and Nicole Brewster—calling themselves Eight Prime—have dedicated themselves to the task of raising funds to buy a bus for an underprivileged children's group known as the Junior Explorers and donating the vehicle in Kurt's memory. It is a staggering undertaking for eight unassisted teens, yet taking on the seemingly impossible is nothing new for group leader Altmann.

"I saw the Junior Explorers as a way to make a difference, of helping people out," said Altmann. "It was a way to show love for my neighbor, too, which is something I really believe in."

Altmann, 16, along with Chris Hobart, 20, founded the Junior Explorers two years ago. The program serves children from poor and broken homes by involving them in a wide range of fun, free activities each Saturday and for two weeks during the summer, when the Junior Explorers will ride their bus to a much-anticipated camp.

In order to make sure the kids have that bus in time, Eight Prime has already undertaken several fund-raising activities, the latest being the construction of an elaborate haunted house in the trackside ComAm storehouse.

"The ancient bus we started out with gave up the ghost last summer," quipped Hobart, gesturing to the spooky scenery being built all around him. "The City Council promised us a new one, but then there was some kind of budget problem and our funding got cut. With any luck, this haunted house will bring us a big step closer to buying that bus on our own."

"I hope a lot of people will come out to support this," Andrews said. "Especially all the people who knew Kurt."

"Kurt had a lot of friends," Conrad added. "He's definitely missed. We know a bus won't bring him back, but it might make people feel a little better to know how much good it's doing."

If you want to help Eight Prime and the Junior Explorers, or if you're simply looking for a spooktacular good time, stop by 153 Oak Street this Thursday, Friday, or Saturday night, from 7 to 11 p.m. Admission is $5 per person, children and adults.

They printed the picture of Eight Prime too, but I'm putting that in my photo album. It's nice to have a photo of us all together—even if it is only one of those grainy newspaper shots. On second thought, maybe I'll pin it up on my bulletin board awhile before I put it in my album.

Mom's going into her office for a couple of hours today, so I'm riding over to the university with her to use the library. The library at CU blows the socks off that dinky public one downtown, and since Mom's a professor she can check out as many books as she wants (and keep them practically forever). Maybe I'll be a professor too someday. Not only is teaching important work, professors get awesome perks: access to all those books, research grants, pensions, sabbaticals, and— best of all—every summer off. As far as careers go, the family business seems hard to beat.

Whoops. Mom's calling.

Things at school were a little less crazy today, although maybe I'm just getting used to it. Strange guys are still flirting with me, and girls I don't even know are looking me over like _they're_ judging the finals. When I think about dropping out of the contest now, though, I have to wonder if there would be that much to gain. Everyone already knows I won in St. Louis, so I might just be kissing off a scholarship for nothing. Besides, Nicole and Miguel would have a fit.

The way he acts, I'm starting to think Miguel's ego gets some sort of boost out of having me model. [For the record, I hope I'm wrong.] On the other hand, if that were true, it seems like he might want somebody to know about us. He never did call on Sunday, but we ate lunch together today and firmed up our plans for the Homecoming Dance (even though that isn't until November). Who's driving and where we're eating and all that is still up in the air, but at least now I'm sure we're going, so I can start looking for a dress.

Jesse was back at school today too, but I only saw him from a distance, walking through the cafeteria. It's funny, but for as much time as the eight of us spend together, we hardly ever hang out at school (unless we're planning something for Eight Prime). We talk to each other a little more now than we used to, but Jesse is still usually with the team, and Melanie with the cheerleaders. Now that I'm thinking about it, I don't even know where Ben hangs out most of the time. Jenna and Peter are always together, but they were friends before Eight Prime, just like Nicole and Courtney. It's weird, but I guess it's also kind of good. If the group was together all the time, we might get sick of each other.

Tomorrow evening we're going to be working at the haunted house again, and whatever doesn't get done we'll have to finish on Wednesday. On Thursday we're opening, so I'm going to put this away now and get busy on my homework. Hopefully I can get far enough ahead that I don't end up buried later.

10/27

Tonight was the first time I've seen the haunted house in the dark, and I have to admit it was pretty spooky. It would be even scarier if you'd never been in the building before, because there aren't any windows and it's really easy to get turned around. Even just standing outside on the pavement is kind of creepy, with all those gnarled-up oaks casting shadows from the moon.

Everyone worked like maniacs tonight, trying to make sure we'd be ready to open in two days. Eight Prime plus Caitlin Conrad, Courtney, and her boyfriend, Jeff, were there, and we finally got all the partition walls up and painted. Courtney and Nicole hung yards of black fabric across the gaps, making a maze of rooms and connecting halls. I mostly worked on tombstones and a crypt I made with painted Styrofoam blocks. I got so busy with that that I didn't see everything everyone else was doing, but I think Jenna, Caitlin, Melanie, and Peter mostly painted scenery. As far as I could tell, Ben was in charge of those cotton spiderweb thingies, because we have them _everywhere_. Miguel, Jesse, and Jeff were the construction crew, and there's nothing left to build now except for wiring the lights and sound. We're going to have a bunch of boom boxes hidden all through the place, playing scary tapes, with just enough light for people to find their way through the maze. It ought to be really, really cool.

Miguel and I drove separate cars and didn't get to talk much because we were busy with different things, but he seemed to be in a much better mood tonight. I got to whisper to him here and there, mostly about the dance. I'm looking forward to that more than ever now. I'd still like to tell our friends about us before then, but at least it makes a deadline for everyone to know by.

Tomorrow Miguel and Peter are going to work on that wiring after school, but the rest of us don't need to be there. We'll all stop by on Thursday afternoon, to make sure we're 100 percent ready, then go home and change for the big opening later that night.

I can't wait!

Hallelujah! I just finished the last of my homework for the week! I asked for early assignments from a couple of my teachers, so now I'm all caught up. It will be a lot more fun working in the haunted house tomorrow when I'm not worrying about precalculus and biology.

I wonder how Miguel and Peter did with the sound effects today? I can't wait to see the place tomorrow with everything all wired.

Well, since I have a couple of free hours, I think I'll watch TV. There's a documentary about the origins of life on PBS tonight, and the preview looked really interesting.

I can't write long because I've got to get my costume on and get over to the haunted house. My parents are chaperoning tonight, so we're all going to grab dinner together first, too. I probably shouldn't even be messing with my journal right now, but I'm so excited that I want to get a few quick things down before we leave.

We were all over at the warehouse earlier (Eight Prime was, I mean), and the place looks <u>fantastic</u>. There wasn't really anything left to do, just little tweaks here and there, and Nicole had some last-minute additions for people's costumes. The coolest thing was to see it completely set up; the tapes sound like wailing and clanking chains, and the lights are dim and half blocked by cobwebs. The entry came out really well too, like the lobby of some ancient, abandoned theater. Miguel's going to be working in the crypt tonight, and that's all finished, with a fake coffin and everything. I'm going to be in this kind of haunted castle room, and Melanie's wearing a skull mask in a black-and-white room with a strobe light. We've got dummies made of stuffed clothes propped around in places too, just to make it harder for people to tell what's real and what's fake. It ought to be really scary for the people who come. I'm actually kind of glad I'm working in it instead of running through it.

While we were there, this skinny, sick-looking dog wandered in looking for food and Caitlin ended up taking it home. That girl is _so_ quiet that I think everyone was amazed when she yelled at Jesse for trying to scare it off. Jesse was amazed, that's for sure; he practically froze on the spot. I could never bring home a stray—not living in an upstairs condo with all of us gone so much. I'm glad Caitlin took it, though. I hope she finds it a home.

Okay, I have a lot of makeup to do and it might take me a few tries to get it right so I'd better get started. This is going to be so fun! I love doing Halloween makeup.

[Hey, here's a random thought: Maybe when I model I should just pretend it's Halloween.]

Tonight was a disaster—completely awful. I wish I had just stayed home. I know I should be happier about the haunted house being such a big success, but that got kind of overshadowed by the fact that Miguel and I had a huge fight and broke up before it even started. The weirdest thing is, I feel like I ought to be sad about it, but I'm still so mad that I don't even care. I'm never going to get to sleep tonight, though, so I might as well write about what happened. [Although, for the record, this is another of those things I can't imagine wanting to remember later. When I started keeping a journal in middle school, it seems like I had a lot less bad stuff to record.]

It all started when I finally realized that if I couldn't bring Miguel to meet my parents, tonight was the perfect chance to take my parents to meet him. I was really excited when we all drove up to the warehouse—about everyone finally meeting and about opening night. My dad parked a block away, to leave room for other cars, and I imagined what the place would look like when the whole curb was filled and a long line of people stood outside the door.

"I wish we could help on the other nights too," Dad said, but he has stuff he has to prepare for school, and on Halloween at least one person has to be at home for the trick-or-treaters.

"I _might_ be able to get someone to take my seminar tomorrow night," Mom offered. "Half my students will cut class anyway with all the parties going on."

"No. One night's enough," I assured them. "We have plenty of chaperones. I mostly just wanted you both to see it."

Which wasn't _exactly_ true, because even though we do have plenty of chaperones, I did have that little ulterior motive. Miguel might have managed to get out of brunch, but I figured I had him trapped this time. We were all on the same piece of property, and he didn't even know it.

Nicole and Peter greeted us in the entry. "Cool costume!" Peter said. "You look fantastic."

"Yeah," Nicole said gloomily. "I wish I'd thought of that."

I don't know why it matters who thought of it, but I _was_ pretty happy with my costume (until later, when Miguel wrecked everything). I had that gold satin dress with the lace shawl draped across my back. My hair was done in ringlets held off my face with combs. But the whole rest of my costume was makeup. I used pancake foundation to take the color out of my face, then fooled around with some other stuff until my skin was almost bluish. The lipstick I used was dark red. But the best part was these two fake puncture wounds I made on my neck, spaced like they were made by vampire fangs. They came out looking so real I almost couldn't believe I had made them myself. I even had fake blood trickling down to my collarbone.

"Thanks," I said, happy they liked it. "I thought that with Jesse being a vampire, I might as well dress up like—"

"—he bit you," Nicole finished for me. She was dressed like a cross between Morticia and Elvira, in a tight, low-cut black dress with a long black-and-gray-striped wig. Peter was dressed simply in black, but he had more stuff to put on later for haunting the graveyard. His first job was organizing the chaperones, though, so I introduced him to my parents and took off to find Miguel. I knew I had to hurry, because people were already starting to line up outside for tickets. There was still half an hour before opening, though, so if Miguel had simply acted normal we would have had plenty of time. What I forgot was, he never acts normal.

When I found him in his crypt, he was fussing with the lights. "Hi!" I said hurriedly. "What are you doing?"

"Trying to get this to shine on the coffin." He stepped down off an overturned crate and got a look at me. "Why, you look downright edible," he teased.

"And you're enough to make a girl lose her appetite," I joked back. His costume is probably the best one in the place, but there's no denying it's totally gross. Since his job is to lie in the coffin, Nicole dressed him like a body somebody dug up. His pants and shirt are shredded to look decayed, and he wears this streaky brown and gray makeup all over his skin. His hair's full of dirt and leaves, and one side of his face has a mask that looks like flesh falling off the bone. That alone should be enough to turn anyone's stomach, but the plastic worms and leeches hanging from his jaw and arms really up the revulsion factor.

"You're going to scare the kids to death," I told him.

"Do you think so?" he asked hopefully.

"You're scaring me."

"I'll show you scary," he said, grabbing my waist. I could tell he was going to kiss me, and we didn't have time for that.

"Miguel!" I protested, skipping out of his reach. "You're going to mess up our makeup."

"_Our_ makeup? I never thought I'd hear that excuse," he grumbled, returning to his lighting— which was really _not_ what I wanted him doing right then.

"What's wrong with the lights?" I asked. "They look all right to me."

"No, they're all wrong. I want this one to shine over there," he said, pointing off to a corner. "And this one down on me. It'll be scarier that way."

"Well, can't it wait a minute? There's someone I want you to meet."

His expression got instantly suspicious, almost like he'd already guessed. "Who?"

"My parents!" I was still foolish enough to be pretty happy about the whole thing at that point. I actually thought I was smart to surprise him, because that way the introductions would be over before he had time to stress about it. "They're dying to meet you," I added, even though we hadn't actually discussed them meeting him there tonight — luckily. I just meant in general.

"Now? Here?" he demanded. "I can't meet them now."

"Why not?"

"I'm busy, for one thing."

"There's nothing wrong with those lights," I said, getting impatient.

"They're not right, Leah. I have to fix them."

"Fix them in a minute, then. It's not like we're going to be outside talking all night."

"I told you, I don't have time. Besides, I'd rather

not meet your parents for the first time when I'm dressed like a half-decayed corpse."

I tried to tell him they wouldn't care, but I don't think he was even listening. He said he would be embarrassed, which is crazy. What does he think? That they've never seen a Halloween costume before?

And then he made a big mistake. "I'm not having this conversation anymore," he said, turning his back on me. "I'm too busy, and that's that."

I couldn't believe he would treat me that way. I was so mad I almost couldn't breathe. I don't know if it was his attitude, or his tone of voice, or just the way he turned his back, but whatever it was, I totally lost it. "You don't _want_ to meet them!" I accused. "Why don't you be a man and admit it instead of blaming it on the stupid lights?"

"I don't want to meet them _now_," he said, wheeling back around. "And I already said that, so what's to admit? What's your problem tonight anyway?"

"My problem is you!" I almost shouted. "I'm sick of your secrets and childish behavior! I've never known anyone who could make a bigger deal out of something so insignificant."

"You're right," he said. "It _is_ insignificant. So why don't you drop it for once? Believe it or not, the world will keep turning if we don't meet each other's parents. You're obsessed with this, Leah, I swear."

"I'm obsessed?" I flung back. "I must have been _possessed_ to ever go out with you."

"Knock it off, Leah," he said. I was getting loud, and I could tell he was worried that people would hear me.

"Oh, I'll knock it off all right," I said, even louder. "I'll knock it off when you march your butt outside and say hello to my parents."

"I'm not going to, so drop it," he said.

I just stared at him. He was like this total stranger—someone I didn't know, and didn't _want_ to know. That dress I was wearing has one of those tight, lace-up bodices, and suddenly I understood why Victorian women were always fainting. My chest was heaving worse than the cover of one of those romance novels.

"You know what, Miguel?" I said. "I _will_ drop it. And I'm dropping you, too. I never want to see you again!"

"Aw, come on. You don't mean that," he said. He started to climb down off his crate, but I was so mad I just turned and ran out of there.

So that's it, I guess. It's over. If he was upset, if he cared at all, he could have come and apologized. But he didn't. In fact, I could hear him howling and terrifying people in his crypt all night long, like he was having the time of his life.

I really thought I meant more to him, but fine. If

he doesn't care, then I don't care either. Everything ends sometime.

This has been the worst night ever. I'm looking back on what I wrote yesterday and I can't even believe I said that. Especially since an hour later I was sobbing into my pillow like a little girl. Of _course_ I care about Miguel. I love him. And even though we've never actually said those words to each other, I thought he loved me, too. I feel physically sick right now, and I know it's only because I'm so miserable.

Seeing him at the haunted house tonight and not talking to him, not even looking at him, was the hardest thing I've ever had to do. I was crying off and on all night; the only thing that saved me is how dark that place is—and the fact that most of my makeup goes on my neck. I just don't understand how I could go from not caring if I ever saw him again to aching for him like this so fast. I usually make a decision and stick to it. I usually _know_ what I want.

The worst part was working so close to him that I could hear his voice. Every time people went through the crypt, Miguel would give a yell, and there'd be all this frantic screaming. The haunted house was even busier than last night, too, since it wasn't a school night tonight. A bunch of the

Wildcats turned out in support of Kurt, and there were a ton of kids there from the junior high. I was glad the rest of Eight Prime was too busy to talk to me much, though, because if any of them had tried to carry on a conversation, I probably would have started sobbing. About the only person I talked to for more than a minute was Ben, and since he usually makes me want to laugh, everything balanced out.

Ben's dressing as a werewolf for the haunted house (his and Nicole's version of one, anyway), with a brown wig, fangs, and glue-on fur on his face and hands. The effect would probably be a lot scarier minus the glasses, but he insists he can't see without them. He came running into my castle about when the crowd was peaking, asking if I'd seen the huge line outside.

"What are you doing here?" I said. "I thought you were working with Peter in the graveyard."

"Chris is back there now and he's giving everybody heart attacks," Ben reported.

That wasn't hard to imagine. Chris was wearing a white hockey mask, and seeing him jump out from behind one of those oversized tombstones <u>could</u> give a person heart trouble.

"So then what are Courtney and Jeff doing?" I asked. It wasn't that I was trying to get rid of him so much as I wanted to be alone.

"Courtney's helping Nicole, and Jeff's chained

himself to a wall back there. He's acting like we caught him going through and now we're torturing him or something." Ben shuddered. "Creepy."

I heard another group coming through, so I told Ben he had to hide. He crouched in a dark corner while I went into my routine. I discovered last night that what scares people most with my costume is when I just stand there with my head lolled back and my eyes glazing over. When they get real close, I moan and sway on my feet a little. This group was all younger girls, half giggly and half terrified.

"Yuck," one of them said, spotting me. "Look at her."

[For the record, I got a lot of that. It's pretty safe to say that no one even thought about recognizing Missouri's newest U.S. Girl.]

"Is she real?" someone else whispered.

I lurched in their direction and everyone backed up.

Then Ben decided to give it a shot. All of a sudden, he lets out this bloodcurdling howl and comes leaping out of his hiding place. The girls whirled around in a panic to see him clawing the air. One of them actually screamed. Then he walked out farther into the light and they started laughing instead.

"A werewolf in glasses? How lame!" one girl scoffed.

Ben stopped clawing, offended. "Werewolves can wear glasses," he said.

"Can not!" they giggled back.

"Can so! What if the person who gets bit and turns <u>into</u> a werewolf wears glasses? They're still going to wear them, right? What are they going to do? Take them off with their claws? They might poke out their own eye!"

By then the girls were laughing too hard to debate him, so I had to intervene. "Good argument, Ben," I said, "but I think we're killing the mood. You girls need to keep moving, before the next group comes in." I waved them through and off they went, laughing all the way.

"I just don't understand it," Ben said when they had gone. "No one's laughing at <u>Miguel</u>."

As if to prove him right, just then hysterical screaming broke out from the very same group of girls. We knew they were in the crypt.

"See?" Ben demanded.

I told him he should try to find a place where he didn't need to see and put his glasses in his pocket, but that he couldn't stay there with me. I was already at the end of my rope, and the fact that our costumes made no sense together gave me a good excuse for moving him along. Ben said he was going to go help Melanie, which made even less sense considering her entirely black-and-white theme, but I decided to let her deal with that.

I have enough problems.

I still can't believe I broke up with Miguel! What was I thinking? I just got so angry when he refused to meet Mom and Dad that I barely knew what I was saying. I thought about apologizing tonight, but the one time he looked at me, when everyone got together right before opening, his eyes were so cold that it gave me the shivers. I could tell he wouldn't be accepting apologies, even if I was brave enough to try one. Which I wasn't.

Maybe I don't deserve to have him back, after the way I acted. How could he ever trust me, knowing I could go off the deep end again at any minute? What really upsets me is, I _never_ act like that. But somehow Miguel brings out these sides of me I never knew were there. The two of us just aren't very compatible. I mean, we usually get along, but we're two completely different people. I don't even know what he's thinking half the time (mostly because he's so tight-lipped about everything that matters).

I'd probably be better off right now if I'd never even met him. I'm _sure_ I'd be better off if I hadn't started everything by kissing him up at the lake. I was so mad at him that day, until he told me how his father had died of cancer, and how he couldn't believe in God anymore because of it. I thought he was acting like a total child, until I found out that he and Kurt had been altar boys together and as far as Miguel was concerned Kurt's death counted as strike two. When I learned that, it was like he went from this sullen, annoying boy to someone I could love, all in an instant.

And last night, for a couple of minutes, he switched back to that first guy again. I guess I shouldn't have been so surprised. People aren't perfect. Maybe I could have been more understanding. I might even have overreacted.

I guess it's too late now.

Halloween

It's Halloween. So what? I'll be glad when this is all over so I can have five minutes to myself. Not only is this the last night of the haunted house, I just got back from helping Eight Prime take the Junior Explorers trick-or-treating downtown. The merchant association put on a costume parade in the morning, and afterward all the kids got to go around collecting some daytime candy. Miguel showed up pretty early, considering it's Saturday, but he's still acting like I don't exist.

It just hurts so bad to be near him now. It's like I still have the same amount of emotion, but now it turns against me. Instead of being happy when I see him, it feels like I can't even breathe. I mostly hung out with Priscilla and Elton, and Miguel mostly watched things from a distance. I guess I'm glad now that we _didn't_ tell anyone about us, because it would only make things harder. It's ironic, in a way—my wanting everyone to know is what broke us apart. If it wasn't so sad, it would be kind of funny.

I'm not laughing, believe me.

At least Jesse was in a good mood today, because Coach Davis is going to let him start practicing with the team again on Monday. He and his little friend Jason were running around like two thugs in cowboy hats, having a blast. I hope Jesse realizes that kid idolizes him. He could pay a little more attention to the kind of example he sets from now on.

Not that I'm any genius on proper behavior. I wish I didn't even have to go tonight. Every time I see him, it's like a knife right through my heart.

This has been the best night ever! Miguel and I made up!!!

Things started out the same, with us ignoring each other. I was so upset I didn't even see how I'd get through the night. But then Miguel talked to Dana Fraser out in the parking lot, and I guess seeing how hard she's taking losing Kurt really got to him. He said he started thinking about how he'd feel if I died and it made our fight seem so insignificant. He came running into my castle, hollering for me, and just hearing him say my name again made my heart start pounding like crazy.

"Leah, I'm sorry," he blurted out before I could say a word. "I was an idiot — a total jerk. I don't know what got into me."

"But why — " I started to ask.

"I don't know why! I only know I can't lose you. Not like this." And that's when he said it — those three little words: "I love you, Leah."

I couldn't help it. I was so happy I just started bawling. "I love you, too," I sobbed, throwing myself into his arms. "Oh, Miguel, I missed you so much. You have no idea."

He said he thought he did, and we agreed to never fight again. "I've just been so on edge lately," he explained. "My mom's kind of sick, but that doesn't excuse my being such a jerk."

When I heard that, I stopped crying and asked what was wrong, because I know how much she means to him. [Which, for the record, is <u>one</u> thing we have in common: Neither of us is ashamed to admit that we really love our parents.]

"It's her kidneys," he told me. "I worry about her sometimes, and I guess it got to me."

"Is it serious?" I asked. I don't know what all can go wrong with kidneys, but I know you need them to stay alive, so I got a little scared when he said that.

To my relief, he shook his head. "They can fix it," he said. "She'll be fine."

I started to hug him again, but just then a loud scream let us know another group was coming through. I tensed up instinctively and Miguel dropped his arms. And that's when I realized that we were doing it again, not letting anyone see us touching. I reached out and put my hand on his arm. "If we're going to be together, I can't do this anymore," I said. "I'm tired of sneaking around, pretending I barely know you. If I'm going to be your girlfriend, I want everyone to know it."

"Do you mean Eight Prime and _everyone_?" he asked.

"Everyone," I repeated.

"Might as well start now, then," he said with a smile. And then he kissed me, right as this rowdy group of junior-high kids ran screaming into the room.

"Ooh, sick!" one of the guys yelled. "That chick's letting a dead guy kiss her!"

"Unh-uh," a girl told him scornfully. "He's biting her. Look at her neck."

"That's from a vampire, stupid. That dude's not a vampire."

"Then why is he biting her?"

There was more of that type of arguing, which, needless to say, wasn't very romantic, but I can't say I paid much attention. It was just so good to be back in Miguel's arms, kissing him again. I felt like I was home, and the knowledge of how close I'd come to losing him made me hang on twice as tight.

"Is that out in the open enough for you?" he teased when he finally let me go. "Should we go do that in front of Eight Prime?"

I believe he would have, too, but everyone was working and there was still a big line outside so we decided to tell our friends after we closed. I did grab the opportunity to make one more thing clear, though, and that was that as far as I was concerned "everyone" included our parents.

"Everyone is going to know," he assured me. "I'll get one of those planes to drag a banner over school if it'll make you feel better."

Wouldn't that be something? I'd be tempted to hold him to it if it wouldn't be so expensive.

Later, after the haunted house was over, we finally did tell Eight Prime. Everyone else was by the entrance counting money when the two of us walked up.

"Miguel and I have something to say," I announced.

They all seemed to notice us holding hands at the same instant.

"We're together," Miguel said simply.

Nicole jumped up from the crate she was sitting on, practically knocking it over. I think it's safe to say she had no clue until that moment. "Congratulations!" she screamed. "Oh, you guys, that's so great! Wow, I'm so happy for you!"

"Yes, congratulations," Melanie chimed in, as if she didn't already know. I have to hand it to her; she kept that secret until the end. Everyone else kind of smiled and nodded, but Nicole was the only one who truly seemed surprised. Maybe Miguel and I weren't quite as sneaky as we'd thought, but I don't care anymore. It feels fantastic to finally have everything out in the open.

We never did get the money counted after that. It was late, and everyone was tired. We have to go back to the warehouse tomorrow to clean the place up anyway, so we decided to count the money then. Peter will bring our whole haul, and we can see what we made over all three nights. We're supposed to meet at two (and as tired as I am right now, I might sleep until 1:30). I'm practically falling asleep while I'm writing this, but I'm so happy that I want to make sure to get everything down. This is one part of the record that I _definitely_ want to remember. When Miguel and I walked out of the warehouse tonight, holding hands for the whole world to see, I felt like I'd been set free. No more secrets!

Well, except for that one little thing. In his car, I actually almost told him about spying on him that time. I am _so_ ashamed of that. I'd love to get it off my chest and start with a clean slate, but I'm just not sure he'd understand. Miguel's a private person and what I did invaded his trust. So I'm afraid that's one little secret I'll have to keep. There's no way he could ever find out unless I told him, and it's not worth risking another fight just to ease my guilty conscience. I don't like it, but that's the way it has to be.

I'll make it up to him somehow. And I've definitely learned my lesson: I'll never do _anything_ like that again. From now on, things between me and Miguel are going to be completely out in the open. This is a new beginning for us, and I feel really lucky to have it.

I just love him so much!

L.R.
+
M.d.R.

11/1

We cleaned up the ComAm warehouse today. What a mess! For a while it seemed like cleaning up was going to take us longer than it had to build things, but once we got the partitions knocked apart the job started going faster. Peter had a plan about the order things should come down in, so that nothing we wanted to keep got broken (like the lights and boom boxes). It worked out pretty well, except that now I'm not only exhausted, I've got this splinter in my thumb I can't get out. As soon as I finish writing this, I'm going to soak in the tub for at least an hour; it ought to come out once my skin softens up.

Once all the sets were cleared out and the trash was in the Dumpster, we swept the whole warehouse and made sure none of those fake cobwebs were left. I actually think we left it in better shape than we found it, except for one little corner where some black paint got spilled. It's just a concrete floor, so hopefully ComAm won't mind too much. Anyway, then the eight of us sat on the floor up front to count our money.

We did fantastic! Our gross was over $4000, although Peter is still trying to figure out our expenses to subtract from that. He said he'd know by the next Eight Prime meeting. Even minus expenses, though, that's a lot of money. I don't think any of us dreamed we could do so well, and the whole group was really happy.

*To me that's the best thing about Eight Prime:
There's something about the eight of us together that's
just bigger than eight separate people. It's like you
add eight together and somehow get twelve, or even
twenty. It's amazing what we get done when we all
work together. Which isn't to say we don't bicker, and
contradict each other, and have completely different
opinions sometimes. But when we all pull in the
same direction, we really get results.*

*I never imagined that day I volunteered to cook
hamburgers that I'd end up part of something so
special, but I'm incredibly glad I did. Even when
Miguel and I were fighting, I didn't think about
leaving Eight Prime, and I don't think he did either.
It's like I was saying before, it's bigger than any of us.*

*I am so glad we're not fighting anymore, though!
Miguel was so sweet today, working with me the
entire time. It's like we have a completely different
relationship, now that we've stopped hiding it. I
thought we were close before, but every time Miguel
touched me today I nearly melted right into him.
Not caring about who might be watching, or glancing
over our shoulders all the time, feels absolutely
amazing, like everything's more real. I can't explain
it exactly, but we've crossed some sort of threshold;
everything's cranked up a notch.*

This is going to sound weird, but I'm actually glad

we broke up, because now that we're back together everything's even better than before. Besides, most couples break up eventually, but how many get back together? I can't help thinking this means we've passed some sort of major test. I don't know, but I do know this: I've never felt about anyone the way I feel about Miguel. I truly believe we'll be together a long, long time.

What Goes Around

Nicole and Courtney have been best friends forever, but Courtney's me-first attitude has gotten out of hand. Nicole is tired of doing backflips to stay in her friend's good graces—and she's not the only one. It was only a matter of time before somebody gave Court a dose of her own medicine . . . but did it have to be on prom night?

Jesse can't believe he was foolish enough to think Melanie would want to be his date for the CCHS prom. He's wasted way too much time dreaming of holding her in his arms—hasn't she made her feelings about him brutally clear?

Melanie tried her hardest to get Nicole on the cheering squad. Maybe that's why she feels so responsible now that her friend didn't make it. First runner-up isn't good for anything. Unless somebody drops out . . .

Coming in October 2000!

volume!